SHOWDOWN IN PECOS TOWN

EVAN MADDOCK—A young attorney caught in the middle of a blood feud when he was forced to defend his brother's accused murderer.

HOWELL TRAINOR—He had been elected state senator with high ideals, only to become the pawn of unscrupulous men and his own trusted aide.

WARREN PRESCOTT—The senator's right-hand man, a master of political chicanery, he was out to steal the entire state of Texas.

KATHLEEN TRAINOR—She loved her father and tried to help him, but she soon discovered that she loved Evan Maddock even more.

AXEL MADDOCK—The patriarch of the Maddock clan, he'd kill every Lindsay he could and brook no meddling from anyone outside or within the family.

The Stagecoach Series
Ask your bookseller for the books you have missed

STAGECOACH STATION 27:

PECOS

Hank Mitchum

Created by the producers of
Wagons West, White Indian, and
Saga of the Southwest.

Chairman of the Board: Lyle Kenyon Engel

BANTAM BOOKS
TORONTO • NEW YORK • LONDON • SYDNEY • AUCKLAND

STAGECOACH STATION 27: PECOS

*A Bantam Book / published by arrangement with
Book Creations, Inc.*

Bantam edition / January 1987

*Produced by Book Creations, Inc.
Chairman of the Board: Lyle Kenyon Engel.*

ISBN 0-553-26193-2

Published simultaneously in the United States and Canada

*Bantam Books are published by Bantam Books, Inc. Its trade-
mark, consisting of the words "Bantam Books" and the por-
trayal of a rooster, is Registered in U.S. Patent and Trademark
Office and in other countries. Marca Registrada. Bantam Books, Inc.,
666 Fifth Avenue, New York, New York 10103.*

PRINTED IN THE UNITED STATES OF AMERICA

KR   0 9 8 7 6 5 4 3 2 1

STAGECOACH STATION 27:

PECOS

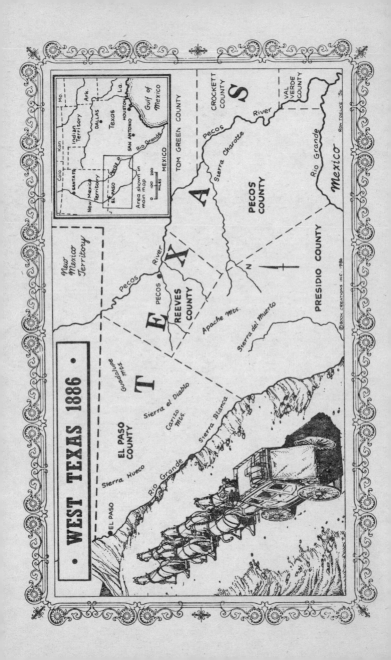

Chapter One

There were few things in this world that Guadalupe Arroyo hated worse than eating trail dust. But at the same time, there was nothing in this world he loved more than money.

Arroyo waved an arm at his cousin Manuel and shouted over the din of the cattle to keep the brutes moving. Then he lifted the sombrero from his head and used his sleeve to mop at the sweat that threatened to drip in his eyes.

Heat and dust . . . it was a way of life when you were a rustler. But in Reeves County, Texas, in May 1886, it was a profitable way of life, thanks to a long-standing feud between two gringo families.

Arroyo and four of his cousins were pushing eighty head of cattle north from the great ranch owned by Axel Maddock. They had made their move in the early morning hours before dawn, when any Maddock hands in the area would be tired and none too alert. They had encountered no trouble. The plan was going smoothly, as it usually did when Ramirio Flores did the thinking.

Flores wasn't out here on the trail, though, in the glare of the sun that grew continually harsher and hotter despite the fact that the morning was still young. Flores was probably asleep in the back room of his cantina, several miles to the west in the city of Pecos. Arroyo felt a touch of resentment because Flores sent him and his cousins to do the real work. At the same time, Arroyo had to give the man some credit. His hands might be soft and unscarred by labor, but his brain was sharp and he had the instincts of a true bandito.

It was Flores who had come up with the idea to take

1

advantage of the Maddock-Lindsay feud. Arroyo knew little and cared less about the origins of the feud, but Flores had put his finger on the most important element.

When old Axel Maddock's riders told him about the missing cattle and that the trail of the stolen steers led north, he would jump to the conclusion that Jubal Lindsay and his men were responsible for the rustling.

Arroyo had to grin as he and his cousins drove the herd across the wagon road leading to Pecos. Up ahead a few miles, they would reach a rocky shelf that ran along the southern edge of the Lindsay ranch. They could turn the cattle west when they reached that shelf, and no one would be able to prove that the steers hadn't continued on to the Lindsay corrals.

In actuality, they would skirt Pecos to the north and wind up at the abandoned cabin that Flores used as the headquarters for his illegal activities. There the brands would be altered, and then the cattle would be driven south to the border.

And then there would be more money in Arroyo's pocket, and that was what mattered.

Arroyo suddenly raised himself in the saddle and shouted at his cousin Francisco, "Watch those strays, you stupid fool!" Fewer cattle meant fewer coins.

Arroyo's grin became more savage when he thought about what would probably happen before the morning was over. Axel Maddock would send his men to recover the missing cattle from the Lindsay ranch. The hands would be edgy, and the Lindsay men would react in kind. There would be shooting, that was a certainty.

And maybe a few more gringos would die. That was nothing, less than nothing, to Guadalupe Arroyo.

He coughed, drew the neckerchief tied over his face a bit tighter about his mouth and nose, and spurred ahead to cut off a steer that wanted to bolt to the side.

Damn the heat and dust, anyway. . . .

Though summer was still a month away, the heat was already starting to make itself felt in the West Texas city of Pecos. People tended to stay inside during the middle of the day rather than expose themselves to the searing rays of the sun. The sky was blue and cloudless most of the time, offering no shade, no relief. But the citizens of Pecos were used to the heat and managed to cope with it, which was about all they could do, except move to a less extreme climate.

Inside the Reeves County courthouse, attorney Evan Maddock rose to make his closing remarks to the judge. In his late twenties, Evan stood six feet tall, with a lean body that was strong and supple. He tried to ignore the trickles of sweat running down his head of thick, dark hair and onto his sun-bronzed face. Despite the temperature, he wore a coat and tie, and his shirt was plastered to his body underneath the coat.

In a deep, resonant voice, Evan said, "Your Honor, the evidence presented in this case is clear enough. My client, Mr. Howard, has proven that he does indeed have title to the disputed property and that such title was registered with the Pecos County land office in Fort Stockton before the formation of Reeves County. He seeks no damages from the defendant, Mr. Green, only an order stating that the land does belong to him and that Mr. Green should remove his cattle. I trust that the court will find in Mr. Howard's favor and so order. Thank you, Your Honor."

The bald-headed judge, equally warm in his robes, looked over at the table where the defendant sat and said, "You got anything else to say, Ezra?"

Ezra Green, a lanky and grizzled rancher, stood up and shook his head. "Reckon not."

"All right, then." The judge leaned back in his chair and unashamedly mopped his forehead with a handkerchief. "The court finds in favor of the plaintiff, Marcus Howard. Ezra, you should've known better than to run your cattle on land you know belongs to someone else. You're lucky he didn't just shoot 'em. You've got a week to move your stock off of there and back to your own spread." The gavel rapped sharply on the bench. "Case closed."

Marcus Howard turned to his attorney with a grin

and pumped Evan's hand. "Thanks, Mr. Maddock. I knew you'd set things straight."

"That's my job," Evan said, returning the smile. After exchanging glares with Ezra Green, Howard left the courtroom, and Evan started gathering up the papers he had spread out on the table in front of him.

"Well, maybe with any luck the two old goats won't shoot each other," said an older man who had pushed through the gate in the railing that divided the spectators from the tables where plaintiff and defendant sat. His name was Billy Chadwell, and he was Evan's partner in the law firm of Chadwell and Maddock. He had been the only spectator for this case, and now he leaned against the table and watched Evan place his papers in a leather case.

"They won't shoot each other," Evan said. "Even a couple of stubborn old mules like those two won't come to killing over a piece of land."

"There have been many killings over that very thing, my friend."

"Not this time, Billy. I had a long talk with Marcus, and he assured me nothing like that would happen."

Billy Chadwell nodded. "I hope you're right."

The judge had stood up and come down from behind the bench, and now he said, "Could I have a word with you, Mr. Chadwell?"

Chadwell turned and said, "Certainly, Your Honor." He went across the room and joined the judge at the door leading into his chambers.

The judge inclined his head toward Evan and said in a low voice, "That's quite a partner you've got there. A little more formal than what I've gotten used to out here, but very effective. The way he's been handling cases the past couple years, he acts like some big-city attorney."

Billy Chadwell grinned and puffed his chest with pride. "I taught Evan everything he knows," he said.

"Then teach him to relax a little," the judge admonished. "I deal every day with ranchers and cowhands and storekeepers and old shysters like you, and then he comes into my courtroom and reminds me how things are supposed to be in a court of law."

Chadwell nodded. "I'll have a talk with him."

Not that it'll do any good, he added to himself. Evan Maddock took the law very seriously, and Chadwell didn't know if the younger man could approach it any other way.

Chadwell rejoined Evan. "How about a drink to celebrate another victory for the law firm of Chadwell and Maddock?" he asked.

Evan smiled. "Don't mind if I do."

The two attorneys walked down the hall from the courtroom and out the front door of the massive sandstone courthouse that sat in the middle of the town square. The courthouse was the most impressive structure in town. Most of the other buildings were only one story, though some of the businesses sported false two-story fronts. The hotels were larger, as was Willie Koehler's General Merchandise Emporium. The buildings on the fringes of the city were mostly low, flat-roofed adobes. Just beyond them to the east, the Pecos River flowed through a broad, shallow valley spanned by the railroad bridge that had brought life and commerce to the new city of Pecos.

The sun's glare was harsh, and both men were glad when they had crossed the courthouse lawn and the street and reached the shade of the sidewalk. The Orient Saloon and Hotel was less than two blocks away, and they strolled toward it slowly, not wanting to exert themselves too much in the afternoon heat.

They made an unlikely pair as they sauntered along the sidewalk. Evan Maddock, considerably younger than his partner, was also much taller than Billy Chadwell. Despite Evan's youth, his thick black hair was starting to show some gray, as was the heavy mustache that partially obscured his wide mouth. The mustache made him appear somewhat solemn, almost menacing. But when he smiled, as he did now at a jocular comment from his partner, he didn't appear threatening at all.

It would be hard to imagine Billy Chadwell ever looking threatening, although in his earlier days he had belied that image as an Army scout and Indian fighter. He was short and thick-waisted now, with a broad, florid, friendly face topped with curly gray hair. In his rumpled town clothes he looked more like a whiskey drummer than a successful lawyer. He had lived all of his fifty-six years on the frontier, knocking around from place to place and occupation to occupation before settling on Pecos and the law, and he had seen some hard times and some hard men.

There was one thing he had in common with the drummer he resembled—there was nothing he enjoyed more than a drink of good smooth whiskey. Billy Chadwell's two favorite places in the world were a courtroom and a smoky saloon.

There were plenty of saloons in Pecos for a man to choose from. When the railroad had come through, bringing the city into existence, the first businesses established had been tent saloons with rough plank bars. The railroad workers were the first patrons at the saloons, but the cowhands from the surrounding ranches kept the drinking places in business. The tent saloons were all gone now, but Pecos still boasted at least two dozen saloons, ranging from hole-in-the-wall dives to Mexican cantinas to the elegant confines of the bar at the Orient Hotel.

As they pushed through the swinging doors of the Orient Saloon, Evan yanked loose the knot in his string tie, pulled it off, and stuffed it into his pants pocket. The shadowy saloon was pleasantly cool. A bar ran the length of the back wall, and at the left end of the bar was the arched entrance to the hotel that was in the other half of the big corner building. The floor was of brightly polished hardwood planks with only a light coating of sawdust. Several tables were scattered around the large room, none of them too close to any of the others; patrons of the Orient liked a little elbowroom when they were doing their drinking and card playing. The back bar was lined with an assortment of bottles that caught the light from the street and sent it back in scintillating sparkles. Above the bottles was a large mirror. Also adorning the walls were the inevitable nude in a gilt frame and several sets of pronghorn antlers. To the right of the bar, a set of stairs led upward, so that hotel guests could return to their rooms without having to go back through the lobby. The Orient Saloon and Hotel was the pride of Pecos.

Evan and Chadwell crossed the room, pulled out chairs, and sat down at a vacant table. Chadwell lifted a hand to signal the bartender, who came to the table a couple of minutes later with a bottle and two glasses. The saloon was busy without being crowded, and the bartender had time only for a quick, "Howdy, Billy, Evan," and a nod before he had to get back to wait on another customer.

Chadwell pulled the cork from the neck of the bottle and smiled at the hollow popping sound. "What a lovely melody," he said as he poured the amber liquid into their glasses. He set the bottle down, lifted his glass, and clinked it against Evan's. "Here's to the law."

"To the law," Evan said. He sipped the whiskey appreciatively and then went on, "That courtroom was like an oven today."

"Legal dignity does tend to be a little stifling sometimes. Especially in this part of the country."

Evan slipped out of his coat, draped it over the back of the chair, and stretched out his long legs, crossing his booted feet at the ankles.

Chadwell looked down into his drink for a moment and then raised his gaze to meet Evan's eyes. "You did a good job in there today, Evan. Makes me proud to have you as a partner."

"I'm proud to be your partner, Billy. You know how much I appreciate everything you've done for me since . . . well, since my folks died."

Chadwell waved a hand, uncomfortable at the expression of Evan's gratitude. "Don't you worry about that," he said. "I just wanted to tell you that you don't have to take everything quite so seriously. Folks around here aren't used to that. And I'm not talking now just about the practice of law. It's more a matter of the way you look at things, like . . . well, do you ever see anything worth smiling at?"

Evan lifted his glass. "Hell, Billy, I smiled just now when I got a taste of this. How much do you have to tip the bartender to get the good stuff instead of the regular bar whiskey?"

"That's between him and me," Chadwell said hastily. "I'm just trying to tell you to relax a little, Evan."

He broke off when he saw that the younger man was no longer paying any attention to him. Evan was looking at the swinging doors and at the man who had just come through them.

The family resemblance was obvious right away, even though Johnny Maddock was eight years younger than Evan, barely out of his teens, in fact. He was more power-fully built than Evan, with broad shoulders and narrow hips, and he wore a handlebar mustache that gave him a certain rakish air. His hat was black and flat-brimmed, its band studded with silver disks. A pearl-handled Colt rode low on his left hip in a hand-tooled holster. It was the kind of weapon worn by a man who was fast with a gun—or who at least fancied himself to be.

In point of fact, Johnny *was* fast with a gun. That was one of the reasons his older brother was frowning at him as he made his way across to the bar.

Johnny had a big grin on his face, and his step was just unsteady enough to tell Evan that he had already been drinking. Evan watched intently as Johnny slapped a palm on the bar and demanded whiskey.

From across the table, Billy Chadwell said in a low voice, "I wouldn't worry about it, Evan. You know how kids are."

"I know what Johnny's like." Evan grunted.

The bartender placed the glass of whiskey in front of Johnny, who lifted it, contemplated the liquor for a sec-ond, and then tossed it down. As he turned away from the bar and wiped the back of his hand across his mouth, he spotted Evan and Chadwell.

Johnny's face broke into a big grin. "Howdy, Evan," he called and then started over toward them. His footsteps weren't any more erratic than when he had entered the saloon, but they weren't any steadier, either.

"Thought you were out at the ranch getting some

fences mended," Evan said, his voice full of reproach, as Johnny came up to the table.

"Too hot for that," Johnny answered with a casual flip of his hand.

"It won't be getting much cooler before fall," Evan pointed out.

Johnny didn't make any reply but instead turned to the older man and said, "Howdy, Mr. Chadwell. You and my big brother won any cases lately?"

"As a matter of fact, one of Evan's clients received a judgment in his favor just a few minutes ago," Chadwell told him. He was clearly unsure what to do, if anything, about the tension between the two brothers.

"Well, good for Evan," Johnny said. His slightly bleary gaze landed on the nearly full bottle on the table. "Anybody gonna offer a man a drink around here?"

Evan picked up the cork and shoved it firmly back into the neck of the bottle. "Looks to me like there's been enough drinking today."

"No such thing." Johnny shrugged. "But if you don't want to share . . ."

He turned away from the table and went back to the bar as Evan stared broodingly at his back. After a long moment, Evan sighed heavily and said, "Sometimes I don't know what's going to happen to that boy."

"He comes from good stock," Chadwell said pointedly. "He'll turn out fine, given time. Look at his big brother."

Evan smiled slightly, ruefully, and then shook his head. "I don't know. It's been mighty hard, trying to help him and Ted grow up. Since Pa and the other boys died . . ."

Evan let his voice trail off, and his mind went back to the deaths of his father and the other two Maddock sons. There had been five boys in the family, Evan being the oldest. Then had come Nathan and William and Johnny and Ted. Now Nathan and William were gone, along with their father, and Evan could still vividly remember how their bodies had looked, bloody and bullet torn.

It was a memory he knew would never leave him.

But it was one he would have to live with, just as he would have to live with the memory of his mother losing the will to live after the killing of her husband and two of her sons. She hadn't been a weak woman—no woman could live on the frontier, raise a family, and make a marriage work for over twenty-five years if she were weak—but something had happened after the deaths. The ability she had always had to throw off any illness had deserted her, as though it were too much of an effort to do battle against the fever when it came and took hold of her. She had wasted away quickly, and when death had claimed her, the sons left behind had hardly been able to recognize her drawn, faded features.

That had left Evan with a ranch to run and his two youngest brothers to raise. Evan was as good a cowhand as any, or at least he had been at one time, but he had been away from the ranch for several years, studying law at the university in Austin, and he had only recently returned to Pecos to go into partnership with Billy Chadwell. Luckily, there was an excellent foreman to take care of the ranch; Evan didn't know what he would have done without the big man named Ignacio Newcomb, known as Nacho. He would have had to give up his law practice, that was certain.

The ranch was in good hands, all right, but he wasn't so sure about Johnny and Ted. Johnny had always had a wild streak in him. In the two years since the deaths of his parents and brothers, that wildness had increased, and Evan didn't seem to be able to do anything to curb it. Ted was only thirteen. There was no way of knowing yet which way he would go with his life. So far, though, he showed a disturbing but not surprising tendency to emulate Johnny.

That damned feud with the Lindsays, Evan thought bitterly. He looked at Johnny, who was standing at the bar knocking back another drink. Evan mentally cursed the whole business. The Maddocks and the Lindsays were the two largest landholders in these parts, and somehow—no one really knew why—a feud had gotten started between them about twenty years back. Evan tried to keep out of it; his job, after all, was to help the law function smoothly.

But his uncle, Axel Maddock, had instilled hatred for the Lindsays in Evan's younger brothers.

Billy Chadwell had kept silent for a few minutes, but now he said, "It doesn't do any good to brood over it, Evan. Your folks wouldn't have wanted it that way."

"They didn't want it the way it turned out, either," Evan said bleakly. "I don't know who's more to blame, the Maddocks or the Lindsays or just this damned country."

"There's nothing wrong with the country," Chadwell said softly. "You can't hold it responsible for the sins and stupidities of the people who live on it. It's there to nurture us if we let it, to take care of us the way we take care of it . . . or to let us kill ourselves if that's what we want." He grinned suddenly and shook his head. "I guess that's the whiskey spouting philosophy."

At the bar, Johnny returned his glass to the hardwood counter with a clatter, spun a coin to the bartender, and turned to walk out. He waved carelessly to Evan and then went through the swinging doors and onto the sidewalk, stepping with the exaggerated caution of a man who's drunk and knows it.

"I worry about the boy," Evan said.

"You worry too much. How about another drink?"

Evan shook his head. "I don't think so. Figured I'd go back to the office and get caught up on some of the paperwork." He added with a grin, "*Somebody's* got to take care of it."

"Have at it, my boy. Wading through paperwork is always valuable experience for an attorney."

Evan stood, picked up his coat, and started to reach into his pocket. Chadwell waved off the gesture and told him that he would take care of the tab. Evan nodded and said, "So long, then."

As Chadwell watched the younger man leave the saloon, there was something very much like fatherly pride in his eyes. From the moment he had befriended Evan Maddock as a young lad, he had known that the boy was going to turn out to be someone special. So far, he hadn't been disappointed. Of course, Evan *did* worry too much, but maybe that wasn't so bad. As Evan had said, somebody had to be serious and take care of the business of the world.

But just now Chadwell had some serious business of his own to attend to, he thought with a smile as he reached for the bottle and uncorked it again.

Ten miles east of Pecos, a stagecoach was rolling along the broad, dusty wagon road. At first glance, it looked like any other Concord coach, but closer study revealed its many refinements. The luggage boot was larger than usual, and the trim, underneath its coating of dust, was pounded and polished brass. The benches inside the coach had been fitted with plush upholstery instead of left bare as they often were. There were fine lace curtains on the windows, along with the standard canvas flaps. This was no ordinary stage-line vehicle. This was a rich man's coach.

Handling the team was a burly, broad-shouldered man in a dark suit. His clothes were dusty and sweat stained, as was the derby perched precariously on his bald head. His grip on the reins was firm and skillful, and the horses, a beautiful team of six matched bays, responded eagerly to his touch.

Gunther Wagner lifted one hand to his hat, plucked the derby from his head, and then used his sleeve to wipe away some of the sweat beading on the bald dome. Gunther had been driving this coach for the last several weeks, and he was a tired man. *If Senator Trainor wasn't so cheap*, he thought, *he would have hired two drivers*.

Inside the coach were four people, two men and two women. The women rode in the forward seat, facing backward, where the effects of the road dust were somewhat diminished, while the men shared the rear seat. The backless bench that usually ran through the center of a coach to provide extra seating had been removed in this one.

Both men were in their forties, though Howell Trainor at forty-eight looked considerably older than Warren Prescott, who was seven years younger. Trainor's silver hair and patrician demeanor made him seem older, while Prescott's thick shock of sandy hair and unlined face concealed his true age. The men had several things in common, though, not the least of which was a life in politics.

Though Howell Trainor had been born to a pioneer family shortly after Texas had won its independence from Mexico and become a republic, his frontier days were far behind him now. When Trainor was a small child, his father had been elected to the Texas senate. The family had moved to Austin, leaving the rough frontier life behind. Things had never been the same for Howell Trainor after that. Growing up, he had been as familiar with the state capitol as he was with his own house. It had been natural that he would gravitate toward a career in politics, especially after what had happened to his father.

Howell Trainor still remembered like it was yesterday how he had come home with his mother one evening to find his father dangling from a rope attached to a ceiling beam in their living room. Trainor was only an adolescent boy at the time, but to this day he could close his eyes and see the way the body had swayed on the noose, the hideous blue-tinged face, the bulging eyes, the swollen tongue. . . .

The elder Trainor had been involved in a graft ring operating in the statehouse, and that involvement was about to be disclosed following an investigation. Fearing that revelation more than he feared death, Howell Trainor's father had chosen that way out, bringing to a sordid end a career that had been largely ineffectual.

Howell Trainor remembered the things that had been said to him by the other children at school, the cruel, callous, brutal remarks about his dead father.

Out of that tragedy had been born resolve.

He had started as an aide to another senator, an old family friend. From there it had been only a short step to running for office on his own. In the more than twenty-five years since then, Howell Trainor's climb up the political ladder had been a steady one. He had held a variety of offices, some elected and some appointed. Always, though, his sights were set on one goal alone. Someday Howell

Trainor was going to be the governor of the great state of Texas.

Now he was convinced that the day was going to be soon. In four months, a general election would be held to choose a new governor, to fill the post now held by old Oxcart John Ireland. Trainor was certain that he was going to win his party's nomination and go on to capture the governorship.

At least that's what Warren Prescott told him, and Warren Prescott had a remarkable record for being right about these things.

Trainor felt quite a debt to Prescott. The man had been his aide and chief adviser for fifteen years now, and he had helped Trainor steer a political career that had always been successful. The disgrace and humiliation of the elder Trainor's suicide was long forgotten; part of the credit for that had to go to the hearty, efficient image that Prescott had helped to create for Howell Trainor.

As a hot wind blew into the coach and brought with it a puff of road dust, though, Trainor thought that maybe just this once, Prescott's idea hadn't been such a good one.

"It's just what you need, Howell," Prescott had said a couple of months earlier in Austin. "Everyone here knows you, but you need more support statewide. You'll be going by stage and won't have to keep to a railroad's route or schedule."

After Trainor had thought it over, the notion of a stagecoach tour across the state had seemed like a good one. They could stop in each major city they came to so that Trainor could make speeches and visit with the local politicos, and if they wanted to stop in some of the smaller towns to drum up some grassroots support, they could do that as well.

The next stop was Pecos, and all of the coach's occupants were ready for a few days of rest there, along with the politics.

So far, the trip had been hardest on the two women. Kathleen Trainor, the senator's daughter, had been determined to go along, though, in order to help her father's campaign in any way she could, and her presence required that she be accompanied by a traveling companion—in this case her maid, Mary Killane. No well-bred young lady from Austin traveled around the state in a stagecoach, even a special chartered one, without the companionship of an older female.

Politics was a way of life to Kathy Trainor, just as it was to her father. She had never known any home except Austin, just as she had never known any parent other than Howell Trainor. Kathy's mother had died when she was two years old, and she had been raised by a succession of nannies and governesses in the twenty years since. She had grown into a beautiful young woman with a trim figure and curly, shoulder-length chestnut hair. Her poise and attractiveness had allowed her to fit right into the social whirl in Austin, and she had served as her father's hostess at a variety of functions since her midteens. Her intelligence and maturity, as well as her beauty, made her quite an asset to his career, and she was well aware of the responsibilities placed on her shoulders.

Mary Killane waved a gloved hand in front of her face as the dust swirled into the coach. The brunette woman, in her thirties and not over five feet tall, was not so much pretty as cute, with a spunky yet forthright personality to match. "My goodness!" she exclaimed. "I don't know why Mr. Wagner can't slow down!"

"I doubt that slowing down would do much good, Mary," Kathy replied. "Not with the way the wind blows out here, anyway."

"Well, perhaps if he slowed down, the coach wouldn't rock quite so much."

"The way I see it, the sooner we get to Pecos the better," Trainor said. He was in a snappish mood, the heat and dust getting to him just as it was the others. He shot a glance of annoyance at Warren Prescott. "I'm ready for a break in this little tour. In fact, I'm just about ready to call the rest of it off."

If Prescott noticed the irritation in Trainor's tone, not a trace of it showed on his smooth, handsome features. "I'm sure we'll make some valuable contacts in Pecos," he said. "Some of these big ranchers out here swing a great deal of influence."

"They'd better," Trainor grumbled.

"Well, when we reach Pecos, I'm still going to speak to Mr. Wagner about his driving," Mary said through gritted teeth.

Kathy smiled, looked out the window, and repressed a laugh. Mary Killane was such a dear—a feisty Irishwoman who never hesitated to speak her mind. From the way she acted sometimes, you'd never know that Mary was a servant. That didn't bother Kathy, however; she looked on Mary as more of a friend than anything else.

And she could just imagine dainty little Mary speaking her mind to brawny Gunther Wagner. It would probably make for an entertaining spectacle.

The coach followed the road toward Pecos, bouncing slightly on its thoroughbraces. It would in all likelihood reach the city in another hour or so. Until then, there was nothing to do but put up with the inconveniences. None of the passengers felt much like talking, so they looked out the windows at the passing landscape, which was flat and featureless for the most part. The ground was covered with scrubby little mesquite trees, but that was the only vegetation except for an occasional clump of twisted brush. Farther on, closer to the life-giving waters of the Pecos River, there would be the grasslands, which helped support the large ranches in the area. Each ranch had to cover a lot of acres to support a decent-sized herd of cattle.

Trainor and Prescott had studied the area somewhat before setting out on the journey, and they knew that the two largest ranches in the county belonged to families named Maddock and Lindsay.

Topping a slight ridge, the coach started down a gradual incline into a broad, shallow valley. Gunther had the team moving at a good clip, and he anticipated no problems during the remaining few miles into Pecos.

Sudden movement to the right caught his eye.

Gunther slowed the team slightly as he watched a group of men on horseback appear on the northern edge of the valley. They were riding hard to the south, toward the road, and they were kicking up quite a cloud of dust.

As he watched the riders approaching, Gunther realized that their route was going to intersect with that of the stage. He pulled back on the reins, slowing the team even more, but he didn't reach for the brake just yet.

Inside the coach, Howell Trainor frowned. "I wonder why we're slowing down."

"Perhaps Mr. Wagner heard us talking," Mary suggested.

Prescott shook his head. "Not over the racket this coach makes." He leaned forward and peered out the window on his side. "I don't see anything out of the ordinary. . . ."

Up on the box, Gunther peered at the horsemen. They were close enough now that he could see them twisting in their saddles, looking behind them. A loud, popping noise came to his ears.

Suddenly, Gunther's eyes widened. Those were gunshots that he heard! He lunged for the brake, yanking at it with one hand while he hauled back on the lines with the other.

Trainor and Prescott were thrown forward as the coach lurched to a stop, but both men were able to regain their balance before they had tumbled to the floor.

"Good Lord!" Howell Trainor raged. "What does that lunatic think he's doing?"

Prescott reached for the door. "I'll find out what's happen—"

He broke off as what sounded like a large angry bee buzzed right by his ear and punched a hole in the opposite door on its way out.

"Someone's shooting at us!" Prescott cried.

Kathy and Mary both gasped loudly, and Trainor became visibly paler.

Prescott reached out and grasped Trainor's arm. "You'd better get down, sir! You, too, ladies!"

Outside, Gunther was struggling to hold the team under control. By now he had spotted a larger second group of riders bolting out of the dust cloud left by their quarry. They were shooting, just like the men they were chasing, and it was the bullets from the second group that now whistled around the coach.

The first bunch of riders flashed across the road in front of the stage, the men whipping and spurring their horses on to greater speed. None of them even cast a glance at the stopped coach; they were too busy riding for their lives away from their pursuers.

Gunther was too busy calming the horses to be frightened or even to think much about the danger he was in, exposed as he was on the box. At least the passengers had a little protection from the body of the coach, though it wasn't going to stop many bullets.

"Whoa!" Gunther yelled at the restless horses. "Whoa, there!"

Kathy and Mary were huddled on the floor inside the coach with Trainor and Prescott crouching above them, shielding them with their bodies. The fear in these close quarters was a tangible thing, pervading the air along with dust, gunshots, and raucous yells from the wild riders.

The second group pounded across the road a scant hundred yards behind the first bunch, and the shouting and blasting of six-guns was finally more than the frightened team could take. Lunging against their harness, the six-horse team bolted.

The leather reins gripped tightly in his hands, Gunther suddenly felt himself being yanked forward, right out of his seat. Seconds later, the coach jerked into motion, and the horses picked up speed. Gunther had to release the reins and grab frantically at the brake lever just to keep from losing his balance and pitching off the driver's box. As his fingers found a hold, he hung on for dear life.

His teeth gritted and his face contorted with effort, Gunther regained his balance and pulled himself back up onto the seat. Once there, however, he could do nothing but hang on, since the leather reins had fallen out of his reach.

The horses wanted only to escape the noises. As their speed increased to a wild-eyed gallop, they left the road

and started across open country, the coach careening reck-
lessly behind them.

The occupants of the coach were tumbled around
madly as it bounced over the rough terrain. Though the
land might look flat to somebody passing by on the road,
there were plenty of little ridges and hollows to make the
ride a violent one.

None of the passengers were quite sure what had
happened, not having seen the riders, but they knew well
enough that the team was running away and that unless
the horses were stopped there was a good chance the
coach would wreck.

Warren Prescott had been thrown to the floor. He
reached up and grasped the edge of the window in the
door, using it for support as he pulled himself up. "Got to
get out there and do something!" he muttered to himself,
unheard in the chaos filling the coach.

He couldn't let anything happen to Howell Trainor.
Not now, not after years of working to get to this position,
not when the things he had always wanted were almost in
his grasp. . . .

The women gasped and cried out as the stage hit a
bump and flung them into the air. They landed roughly on
the floor again.

Prescott was on his feet now, crouching by the door.
He twisted the handle and the door swung open, giving
him an even better view of the ground racing by outside.
Ignoring the danger, he reached up and got a firm grip on
the railing around the top of the coach and then swung a
leg out, searching with his foot for some kind of toehold on
the side of the coach.

He found one on a brass fitting, took hold of the
railing with his other hand, and pulled himself out onto
the side of the coach, kicking the door shut. Dust flew in
his face, grating in his eyes and making it difficult to see.
He edged himself toward the front of the coach, carefully
feeling for toeholds as he held onto the railing. Soon he
could make out the bulk of Gunther Wagner on the box.
He swung a leg up, hooked it over the side of the box, and
awkwardly clambered up next to Gunther.

The burly driver had lost his derby somewhere along the way. He was leaning far forward, holding on to the footrest with one hand and reaching down for the fallen lines, but they were just out of his reach.

It was only a matter of time until disaster struck. Gunther glanced forward and saw a dark line across the ground in front of them. He knew as soon as he saw it that it was a gully, deeper than any they had encountered until now, and it was less than a quarter of a mile ahead.

He looked over at Prescott, a little surprised that the man had risked climbing out of the coach, and yelled over the clatter of the wheels, "Hang onto me!"

"What?" Prescott shouted back.

Gunther straightened up long enough to whip off his jacket and let it go flying. He pointed to the broad leather belt that encircled his thick waist and repeated, "Hang on!"

Prescott reached over and slid his fingers around the belt, locking them in place. "All right!" he shouted to Gunther.

The big driver leaned far over, reaching down for the reins. His weight pulled at Prescott, and Prescott found himself sliding down onto the floor of the box. He braced his knee solidly on the floor and felt pain start to ripple through his arms as they took the strain of Gunther's considerable weight.

Fleeting seconds went by, but to Gunther, faced with the flashing, deadly hooves of the horses only a foot or so from him, they seemed much longer. It would have made more sense, he knew, for him to have lowered Prescott instead of the other way around, but this coach and its team were his responsibility. The fact that Prescott was lighter didn't change that.

He felt Prescott lurch, but the grip on his belt didn't slip. Gunther reached out. The leathers were just inches beyond his outstretched fingertips. Just a little farther . . .

The bouncing lines brushed against his hand. He grabbed desperately and then had them.

"Pull me up!" he cried.

Prescott hauled at the great weight and felt like his

back was going to break. Either that, or his arms were going to be ripped right out of their sockets. One of those things had to happen.

But by then Gunther was able to reach back with his free hand and take hold of the footrest, relieving Prescott of some of the weight. Between the two of them, they got him back up on the box, the leather reins gripped firmly in his fist.

Gunther shook his head to get the sweat out of his eyes, and then using the brake and the reins, he managed to pull the team to a stop. If the horses hadn't been running hard for some time, getting out some of their fear, he doubted if he would have been able to stop them even then.

As the stage creaked to a halt, Gunther and Prescott both looked at the gully only fifteen feet in front of the lead horses. The cut in the earth was a good eight feet deep. If the stage had gone smashing into it, someone would certainly have died.

Gunther swung down from the box and went forward on shaky legs to try to calm the animals more. As Prescott climbed down, the door of the coach popped open and Howell Trainor stepped out.

Trainor's fine suit was disheveled from the jolting he had received, and the pallor of his face was slowly reddening into anger. He stalked toward Gunther and demanded, "Just what the hell did you think you were doing, Wagner?"

Gunther patted the muzzle on one of the lead horses and spoke softly, soothingly to it before turning to face his employer. "Sorry, Mr. Trainor," he mumbled. "They just got away from me when the shooting started."

"I thought you were trying to kill us!" Trainor blustered. "Racing across country that way."

"Wasn't my idea, sir. I can promise you that."

"Well, see that it doesn't happen again," Trainor snapped.

"Yes, sir." Gunther stared off at the horizon rather than reveal what he really felt about Trainor's unjustified abuse.

Prescott had gone to the door of the coach as soon as

he got down off the box. He looked in and asked anxiously, "Are you all right, Kathy?"

Kathy Trainor was picking herself up off the floor, and Mary was helping her. Both women appeared to be unharmed, but each showed the strain of what they had just gone through. Kathy forced a smile and said, "I'm all right, Warren. What about you?"

"I'm fine if you are." Prescott heaved a relieved sigh.

Kathy turned to her companion. "What about you, Mary?"

"I believe I'm all right, thank the Lord. What a ride! I don't believe I've ever been so frightened."

Prescott held out his hand to Kathy. "Both of you had better step out and get some fresh air." When he had helped the two women to disembark, he turned to the driver and said, "Gunther, what exactly happened back there?"

Gunther pointed a blunt finger at a distant plume of dust on the horizon to the south. "Two bunches of riders came charging by shooting at each other. I figure that's them down there."

Now that things were quiet, the occasional faint crack of gunfire came floating to them, but the riders themselves were well out of sight except for their dust.

"I don't know what it was about," Gunther went on. "They were just there all of a sudden, trying to kill each other and spooking my horses at the same time."

"Gunther saved our lives by retrieving the lines," Prescott put in. The big bald man looked embarrassed and clearly wanted not to dwell on that part of the incident.

Howell Trainor, for his part, was still a very frightened man. He had tried to cover up that fear to a certain extent by converting it into anger at Gunther. But deep down he knew what had caused the queasy knot in his stomach: While the horses had been bolting, when he was possibly only seconds away from death himself, Howell Trainor had kept seeing in his mind's eye the contorted face of his father as he swung from the ceiling of a small house in Austin.

For Trainor to die now, before he had reached his

goal, would be totally unacceptable. If that had happened, he would have been as big a failure as his father had been. When the time came—within months now—the governorship was going to taste so very sweet.

"Well," he said. "I suppose we'd better get back on the road and continue on to Pecos. You can find your way back to the road, can't you, Wagner?"

"Yes, sir. I believe I can."

"Let's be at it, then."

The four passengers boarded the stage once more, and Gunther climbed onto the box to get the team carefully turned around. Then he slapped the leather reins on the horses' backs, clucked at them, and said, "Get along, there!"

With rattles and creaks, the coach started to roll toward the road.

Several miles south of the road to Pecos, Jubal Lindsay lifted a callused hand and called a halt. The group of men behind him reined in their horses.

Jubal spat tobacco juice in the dust and ran his fingers through his scruffy red beard. "Reckon those goddamn Maddock hands'll think twice 'fore tryin' to steal any Lindsay stock again," he said.

Jubal watched with rheumy old eyes as the group they had been pursuing vanished farther to the south. They were on Maddock land now, and that made Jubal uncomfortable.

To look at him, one wouldn't think that Jubal Lindsay was a successful rancher. In torn, dirty range clothes, rundown boots, and battered, shapeless hat, he looked more like an old desert rat. But he controlled a considerable amount of land northeast of Pecos.

His men sat quietly in their saddles, grateful for the chance to catch their breath. The chase from the Lindsay ranch had been a hard one. None of them had been hit by the shots fired by old Axel Maddock's men, but they were still hot and tired.

Matt Lindsay, Jubal's son, rode up next to his father. An arrogant grin split his handsome face as he said, "We

really put the run on 'em, didn't we, Pa?" Without waiting
for an answer, he reached into his saddlebag and pulled
out a shiny silver flask. He uncapped it, put it to his lips,
and tilted his head back, his throat working as he took a
long swig of the fiery whiskey.

Jubal glanced over at his son and growled, "Sun
shinin' on the jug'll make a mighty fine target if some
of them Maddock men have doubled back to bushwack
us."

Matt laughed harshly. "That bunch? Hell, they was
too scared to do anything 'cept run on back home!"

Jubal's hand lashed out and slapped the flask from
Matt's grip. It spun through the air and landed on the
sand with a thud, the whiskey inside gurgling out to form
a dark puddle that was quickly sucked up by the thirsty
ground.

Matt jerked back and glared at his father. "What the
hell you do that for, Pa?" he demanded. "That's wastin'
good whiskey!"

"The range is no place for boozin'," Jubal said with a
snarl. "Especially not Maddock range. Now let's get on
back to the ranch."

He wheeled his horse and put the spurs to it. His
men parted, reining their horses aside to let him gallop
through their midst. Then they fell in behind him.

Matt Lindsay hesitated, watching his father's stiff back
as the old man rode away. He glanced at the flask and
then dropped from the saddle to scoop it up. Mounting up
again, he brushed the sand from the flask, recapped it,
and snugged it away in the saddlebag. There was always
more whiskey to replace what had been spilled. He savagely spurred his horse and rode after the others.

As the group approached the road again, they could
see the tracks where the stagecoach had been dragged by
the runaway team. To anyone who could read a trail, the
story was plain, including the fact that the coach had
nearly plunged into the gully. By now it had regained the
road and evidently continued on its way to Pecos. It was
nowhere to be seen.

Matt had moved up through the riders to a spot

beside and just behind his father. Such a place was his
right, since he was the old man's boy. Now he said, "Bet
we scared the hell out of those folks in the stagecoach.
Wonder what the coach was doing out here anyway. Ain't
a regular run through Pecos."

Jubal ignored his son's comment. He wasn't the least
bit interested in any stagecoach, not when there were
Maddock hands around to shoot at.

His father was a cold-hearted old son of a bitch, Matt
Lindsay thought. And that was just fine with him.

Because that was just the kind of son the old man had
raised.

Chapter Two

The law firm of Chadwell and Maddock was located on the second floor of one of Pecos's few two-story buildings, above Willy Koehler's General Merchandise Emporium. There was a private office for Billy Chadwell, and one big room served as reception area, law library, and office for Evan Maddock.

Evan was seated at a table in the big room, law books spread open in front of him and papers scattered around. There were two large windows in the office, both of them overlooking Main Street and both of them open to catch any stray late afternoon breezes.

Evan had been up here working since leaving Billy Chadwell in the Orient Saloon, and he was starting to get tired. He put down the pencil he was using and leaned back in his chair, stretching his arms over his head and listening to his bones creak. Sounded as if he was getting old, he mused.

He heard the rattle of horses coming down the street outside, followed by a man's shout of "Whoa!" His curiosity aroused, Evan pushed his chair back, got up, and went to the window. He leaned his hands on the sill and looked across the street at the scene in front of the hotel.

A stagecoach had just pulled up, which was unusual in itself. It wasn't often that they saw a stage in Pecos, since there wasn't a regular stage line here.

Pecos was a city that owed its existence to the railroad. The Texas and Pacific had begun laying its track through the area only five years before, in 1881, and it had been only natural that a settlement would spring up where the railroad crossed the Pecos River. Since that time, the city had grown at such a rapid rate, along with the northern half of Pecos County, that an election had been held to form a new county, which bore the name Reeves, out of the western part of Pecos County. Pecos City, as it was called then, had won out in a vote to decide the new county seat. It was the beginning of big things for the city, and now anyone passing through the bustling community would not guess at its relative youth.

Evan and his family had owned their ranch long before the town had been built, of course, and he remembered riding as a child with his father through open rangeland where Pecos City had later been built.

Most of the people in Pecos and the surrounding area used the train when they needed to get anywhere a horse couldn't take them. An occasional stage passed through. This one was stopping, though, and it didn't look like a regular stage, Evan saw as he watched from his window.

The driver was alone on the box, no shotgun guard in sight. He looked capable of doing any guarding that needed to be done, however. He was tall and broad and bald-headed, and when he was scowling, as he was now, he looked pretty formidable.

Evan saw the driver swing down from the box and open the door of the coach for the passengers. The first one off the stage was a middle-aged man with silver hair, wearing a fine suit and a short top hat. He looked around, an angry expression on his face, and then strode toward the porch of the hotel.

The next man off the stage was younger than the first. He was equally well dressed, though, and he carried a cream-colored Stetson in his left hand. He turned back to the stage as soon as he had alighted and offered his free hand to the third passenger.

A woman climbed carefully down from the coach with the man's assistance, and Evan Maddock thought that without a doubt she was one of the most beautiful women he had ever seen. She wore a dark blue dress that was trimmed with enough lace to be elegant without being too fancy. A pretty little hat of the same color sat on a thick mass of chestnut hair. Her figure was slender but well curved, and even from across the street, Evan could tell that the bloom of youth colored her cheeks.

There were plenty of pretty women around Pecos, but this newcomer put all of them to shame.

The fourth and final passenger to disembark from the stage was also a woman and was also attractive, but her looks didn't approach the beauty of the younger woman. This lady was in her thirties, a brunette wearing a dark green traveling outfit that was considerably less expensive than the clothes worn by her companion.

All the travelers looked out of place on the dusty streets of Pecos, and Evan couldn't help but wonder what they were doing here. He cast a glance over his shoulder at the paperwork piled up on the table.

There was no question that he really ought to get back to work. On the other hand, strangers didn't come into Pecos every day, especially strangers like these.

Evan went to the door of the office and plucked his hat from a rack just inside the entrance. The paperwork could wait until he had satisfied his curiosity.

The door opened onto a flight of wooden stairs that led down the side of the building. On the wall at the bottom of the stairs was a sign that proudly announced CHADWELL & MADDOCK, ATTORNEYS AT LAW.

As Evan walked past the sign, he felt the old familiar thrill that always coursed through him at the sight of the words. He had had a dream, and he had worked hard to make it a reality. He didn't see anything wrong with taking pride in that.

As he started across the street toward the hotel, he heard a deep, loud voice say, "Where is the sheriff's office? I demand to see the sheriff! We were nearly killed!"

The fear had faded in Howell Trainor during the ride on into Pecos, but the anger had remained and had grown stronger. As he stepped up onto the porch of the hotel, a man who had obviously been watching for their arrival came bustling out with a big smile and an extended hand.

"Senator Trainor?" the man asked. "I'm Norman

Bardwell, the owner of the hotel. Let me say what an honor it is to welcome you to Pecos!"

Trainor let the man grab his hand and pump it a couple of times; he hadn't refused a handshake in years and wasn't going to start now, no matter how angry he was. But as soon as the eager-to-please Bardwell dropped his hand, Trainor demanded that he tell him the where-abouts of the sheriff.

Bardwell blinked in surprise. "I don't understand—" he started to say, but Trainor cut him off. "It's a simple question," Trainor snapped. "Where is the sheriff?"

Bardwell, anxious to smooth over whatever difficulty had his special guest so disturbed, said, "Maybe there's something I can do to help. If you'll just tell me—"

"I told you!" Trainor snapped, his voice rising. "I want to see the sheriff."

Warren Prescott stepped up onto the porch, bringing Kathy and Mary with him. To them, he said, "Why don't you ladies go on inside and get out of this heat? Gunther can bring in the luggage."

He watched with a smile on his face as the two women went into the hotel. Then, still smiling, he turned to where Trainor was glaring at the nonplussed hotel owner.

With practiced smoothness, Prescott insinuated himself between Trainor and Bardwell and said, "We had some trouble out on the road. If you can tell us where to find the sheriff, we'd like to bring it to his attention."

"Some trouble." Trainor snorted. "I tell you, we were nearly killed!"

A tall, dark-haired man with a mustache stepped up onto the porch next to the group. "Excuse me," he said. "I couldn't help overhearing. Maybe I can help."

"Are you the sheriff?" Trainor asked.

"No, sir, my name's Evan Maddock. I'm an attorney."

Trainor shook his head impatiently. "I don't need a lawyer. But if I ever find those men who were doing the shooting, *they'll* need a good lawyer, I promise you!"

"Shooting?" Bardwell swallowed. "Somebody shot at you, Senator?"

Prescott said quickly, "It was more that we were unlucky bystanders. There were two groups of men shooting at each other—"

A gray-haired man in town clothes moved up to the group and interrupted Prescott by saying, "Here now, what's all this? I could hear the commotion clear down at my office."

Evan Maddock said, "Sheriff, these folks ran into a problem out on the road. They've been wanting to talk to you."

Sheriff Issac Ring faced Trainor and Prescott and said, "Well, I'm here. What happened?"

"We were nearly killed!" Trainor said again.

"This is Senator Trainor from Austin," Bardwell put in, speaking to the sheriff. "Ain't you going to do something about what happened to him, Ike?"

"Nobody's told me what that is yet," Sheriff Ring pointed out. He glanced over at Evan. "You know what's going on, Maddock?"

"Not me, Sheriff," Evan said with a shake of his head. "I just got here, too."

Prescott held up his hands to bring the babble of conversation to a halt. "I believe I can explain everything, gentlemen." He paused and saw that the others were waiting for him to go on. He nodded toward his employer. "This is Senator Howell Trainor, and I am his aide, Warren Prescott. Senator Trainor's daughter, Kathleen, and her maid have already gone into the hotel."

"The senator's here to give a speech," Bardwell interjected.

Prescott shot him a sharp glance and went on, "We are on a special tour of the state, and as we were coming toward Pecos, we encountered two groups of men out on the road. One group seemed to be, ah, chasing the other group. Both groups were shooting at each other. Our team spooked and ran away, and our coach almost crashed before the driver got it back under control."

The sheriff had remained silent during Prescott's explanation. He reached up and rubbed a hand over a gray-stubbled lantern jaw. "Anybody hurt?" he asked.

Prescott shook his head. "We were just bounced around a bit."

"A bit!" Trainor exclaimed. "I thought we were all going to die. I never saw such a band of hooligans and roughnecks!"

Strictly speaking, Trainor hadn't seen the riders today, either, but Prescott didn't point that out. Gunther had said that they looked like ordinary cowboys, and he saw no reason to doubt the brawny driver.

"Where'd you say this happened?" Sheriff Ring asked.

Prescott called out to Gunther, who was taking bags out of the luggage boot, "How far out of town were we when the shooting started, Gunther?"

The bald-headed man paused in his work, frowned in concentration, and said, "About ten miles, I'd make it."

"Ten miles east?"

Prescott nodded in answer to Ring's question.

"What direction were these men ridin'?"

"They were headed south," Prescott said.

Evan Maddock had listened intently to what Prescott had to say. He had found out a lot about the newcomers—including the name of the beautiful young woman who had caught his eye from across the street—and that was why he had come over in the first place.

But as Prescott's story unfolded, Evan found an uneasy feeling growing in his stomach. Sheriff Ring made it worse by turning to him and saying, "Sounds like your bunch and the Lindsays are at it again, Maddock."

Trainor's angry glare immediately turned to Evan. "Your bunch?" he said, echoing the sheriff's words. "You mean you have something to do with those ruffians?"

Evan wished Ike Ring had kept his mouth shut. He gave a disgusted shake of his head. "An accident of birth," he said shortly.

Prescott looked like something had occurred to him. "Maddock," he mused. "Would you happen to be related to Axel Maddock?" He knew from his preparation prior to the trip that old Axel Maddock was one of the largest landholders in the county, if not in all of West Texas.

"He's my uncle," Evan said.

"I'd wager that the first bunch of riders you saw were some of Axel's hands," the sheriff said. "Probably strayed up onto Lindsay range for some reason and Jubal was runnin' 'em off when you came along." He clucked his tongue. "Still, can't have folks goin' around shootin' and endangerin' innocent bystanders."

"I should say not," Trainor declared pompously. "What's going on around here, some kind of war?"

Ring looked at Evan and waited to see if the young attorney wanted to answer that question. When Evan didn't say anything, the sheriff said, "You might call it that. The Maddocks and the Lindsays have been feudin' for going on twenty years now. There was a feud a long time before there was even a town here."

Prescott's eyes raked over Evan. "If I may say so, you don't look like the kind of man to be involved in a feud."

"I stay out of it," Evan said. His tone was brusque; he wished the subject had never come up.

"But your family is part of it," Trainor said, his voice shaking with anger. "They nearly got us killed. You're all a bunch of outlaws and roughnecks!"

Evan kept a tight rein on his temper. He didn't like Senator Howell Trainor, didn't like his bluster. But all he said was, "You've got no call to talk like that, Senator. You don't know the situation—"

Gunther had been stacking the luggage from the boot on the hotel porch, but he had heard enough of the conversation to know what was going on. When he heard Trainor's outburst and Evan's tight-lipped response to it, he stepped up on the porch and dropped a big hand on Evan's shoulder.

"You'd better watch the way you talk to the senator, mister," he rumbled.

Evan swung to face him and looked down pointedly at the fingers gripping his shoulder. "And you'd better watch who you grab, friend," he said quietly.

"I ain't your friend." Gunther gave Evan a hard shove that drove him back against one of the posts supporting the porch roof.

Evan bounced off the post and caught his balance.

His fists were clenched, and that was all the invitation that Gunther needed. The bald-headed man started to swing a punch at Evan's head.

Prescott cried, "No, Gunther!" and the sheriff exclaimed, "Hold it there!" And though both of them started forward to try to stop the impending fight, they were too late.

Evan saw the blow coming in plenty of time to duck under it. As Gunther's fist whooshed over his head, Evan stepped in closer and drove a hard right into Gunther's stomach.

Air exploded from Gunther's mouth, and he looked stunned by the force of the punch. Before he could do anything else, Evan brought his left fist up and clipped the big man on the chin, leaving Gunther in perfect position for a looping right that smashed into his jaw and sent him staggering backward, glassy eyed.

Prescott and Ring caught Gunther by the arms and kept him from sprawling on the sidewalk. Gunther shook his head and growled deep in his throat, but Prescott tightened his grip and said, "Come on, Gunther. Leave it alone." His voice was urgent. "We've got to get this luggage into the hotel."

Gunther shook off the hands that held him, but he made no further move toward Evan. He gave the lawyer a hard look that proclaimed louder than any words that this battle might be over but the war had yet to be decided.

Trainor looked like he wanted to say something else to Evan, but Prescott smoothly got him into the hotel before anything else could be said. Gunther resumed unloading the luggage.

Evan turned away from the hotel and went several steps down the sidewalk, Ike Ring at his side. The sheriff looked back over his shoulder at Gunther and commented, "You didn't make any friends back there, Maddock."

"Didn't come over to make friends," Evan said. "Just wanted to see if I could help out!"

The sheriff went on to his office, but Evan paused and looked back also, and he saw something that riveted him to the spot.

The woman from the stage—her name was Kathleen, he recalled—was looking directly at him from one of the hotel windows, and the expression on her face was hard and unfriendly.

Had she seen the brief scuffle? If she had, what had she made of it? Obviously, she wasn't too impressed with what she had seen of Evan Maddock.

He shook his head to get those thoughts out of it. He had more important things to worry about, though just what they were he couldn't quite think of at the moment.

Billy Chadwell sauntered toward him from across the street. He had a cigar in his mouth, which he rolled from one side to the other before saying, "Looked like ol' Howell was in quite a huff."

"You know him?" Evan asked.

Chadwell nodded. "Knew him when I was in the state legislature. I heard that he was making a tour of the state to drum up support in his campaign for governor. Guess that's what he's here for."

Evan looked thoughtful. "I remember him now. He was in the newspaper all the time in Austin when I was going to school there. He was always a busy man, into all sorts of things."

"He's an ambitious man," Chadwell said slowly. "He's wanted to be governor for as far back as I can remember."

"Seems like an awful lot of work to me, trying that hard to get elected."

"It's important to him."

"Well, I'm going back to the office. There's enough work there for *me*."

Chadwell nodded. "I'll be up in a bit."

He watched Evan go back across the street and climb the stairs leading to the law office. Then he glanced at the hotel and thought about Howell Trainor.

An ambitious man, he had called the politician from Austin. Which was the same thing, Chadwell decided, as a dangerous man.

Chapter Three

Sheriff Ring had returned to his office on the ground floor of the courthouse following the arrival of Trainor's party. He had been there about ten minutes when the door opened and Howell Trainor himself stepped into the office.

Ring suppressed a groan. From the tight look of Trainor's face, it was obvious that the politician was still angry and had come to continue raising a ruckus.

Without preamble, Trainor said, "Sheriff, I'd like to know just what you plan to do about what happened this afternoon."

Ike Ring was seated at his desk. He leaned back in his chair and started to put his booted feet up on the desk, but then thought better of it. Trainor seemed to be the sort who would take offense easily.

"Well, now," the sheriff said slowly, "I told you I'd have a talk with Axel Maddock and Jubal Lindsay. I don't think you'll have to worry about them causin' you any more trouble."

Trainor shook his head. "That's not good enough. I want someone in jail for this. If Maddock and Lindsay are responsible, I demand that you arrest them."

Ring's eyes widened as he tried not to show the surprise he felt. "Arrest 'em? I don't know if I can do that, Senator."

"Why not? Are you afraid of them?" Contempt dripped from Trainor's voice.

The legs of Ring's chair thumped on the floor as he sat up abruptly. He put his palms flat on the desk and shoved himself onto his feet.

"I've been sheriff up here for three years," Ring said in a low voice. "Before that I was chief deputy down at Fort Stockton for ten. I don't take kindly to talk like that, Senator."

Trainor saw that he had overstepped his bounds. But it wasn't in him to back down too easily when his temper was up. Over the years he had grown accustomed to people doing what he told them to do.

"Perhaps I misunderstood the situation," he said stiffly. "Is there some reason you can't arrest the men responsible for nearly making my stagecoach crash?"

"A little matter of proof," Ring said, still leaning on the desk. "We're not certain that it *was* Maddock and Lindsay men you saw, likely though it may be. And even if it was, all Axel and Jubal have to do is deny that they had anything to do with it. Lord knows there's enough skirmishes between those two outfits." Ring shook his head. "Nope, just don't think you could make a case."

"It's a miscarriage of justice, that's what it is," Trainor declared. "But if that's the way you feel, Sheriff . . ."

"It is."

"We'll simply have to let the matter ride for the moment, then." Trainor pointed a finger at Ring. "But I'm telling you now, I intend to talk to some of the leaders of this county about finding a man better suited to keep the peace."

Ring nodded slowly, anger smoldering in his eyes. "You just do what you feel like you have to, Senator."

"I shall, I promise you."

With that, Trainor spun on his heel and stalked out of the office.

Down the street at the hotel, Warren Prescott watched as Gunther and one of the hotel porters carried the luggage up the stairs. It was quite a job; Trainor didn't believe in traveling light.

The party had reserved their rooms in advance. Trainor and Kathy had a two-bedroom suite on the second floor, the largest set of rooms in the hotel, in fact. Prescott had booked a single room directly across the hall from the suite. As for the servants, Mary Killane had a small room set aside for her on the ground floor, while Gunther would bunk in the livery barn, where he could keep an eye on the stagecoach.

At the moment, Kathy and Mary were upstairs in the suite, beginning their unpacking. Prescott sauntered over to one of the windows in the genteel little lobby and looked out at the street. They had chosen this hotel rather than the Orient, even though it was smaller and not as luxuriously appointed, because it wasn't combined with a saloon that attracted cowboys and all other kinds of people. This hotel had a small, discreet bar that catered only to its guests, and Prescott was considering paying it a visit.

As he looked down the street, he saw Howell Trainor disappearing into the courthouse. The senator had insisted on continuing his discussion with the sheriff about the incident on the road, and when Prescott had offered to come along, Trainor had angrily refused, saying he could take care of this matter himself.

Prescott sighed. He hated to let Trainor out on his own, especially when he was incensed about something. There was no telling what he would do.

One of the duties of a politician's aide was to make sure his boss didn't do anything to make himself look foolish. *That's a full time job with Howell Trainor*, Prescott thought disgustedly. *If only he knew how often I've smoothed things over for him!*

But there were a lot of things Trainor didn't know. . . .

Prescott turned away from the window and went to the stairs, ascending them to the hallway where the Trainor suite was located.

The door to the suite was open, since Gunther had just carried in the last trunk and deposited it with a thump. As Prescott strolled into the room, Gunther said to Kathy, "Is there anything else I can do for you, ma'am?"

"No, thank you, Gunther, that's fine," Kathy said. "You can go tend the coach and the team now."

"Yes, ma'am." Gunther glanced at Mary Killane, who was standing to the side. "And good day to you, ma'am."

"Good day, Mr. Wagner," Mary said formally.

Prescott stepped aside to let Gunther leave and then said, "I'll help you unpack, Kathy. You can go tend to your own things, Mary."

"Oh, that's not necessary, Warren," Kathy said. "It won't take long to unpack these things, and then Mary can tend to her own luggage."

"I said I would help," Prescott insisted. "You run along, Mary."

If he saw the hurt look Mary gave him at the curt dismissal, he gave no sign of it. He simply stood there, a pleasant smile on his face, until Kathy finally said in a soft voice, "You can go, Mary. I'll take care of this."

"Whatever you say, Miss Kathy."

Mary left the room, and Prescott unobtrusively but firmly shut the door behind her. Still smiling, he turned back to Kathy.

Before he could say anything, she asked, "Why did you do that, Warren? I think you hurt Mary's feelings."

"I didn't mean to," he said. "I just wanted to talk to you alone, Kathy. And I would be glad to help you with your unpacking."

"Oh, no," she replied with a slight smile. "There are certain things in a lady's trunk that a gentleman has no business seeing." Her expression became more serious. "You said you wanted to talk to me alone."

Prescott went to the window of the sitting room and pushed aside the lace curtain to gaze out at the street. Without looking at Kathy, he said, "This afternoon when the stage was running away, I didn't think about what might happen to me if we crashed. I was thinking about you, Kathy. I was worried about you."

Kathy said nervously, "I think we were all worried about each other—"

"No." Prescott swung away from the window to face her. "It was more than that. I realized in that moment of danger . . . just how much you mean to me."

Kathy looked flustered, as though she didn't like the turn that this conversation was threatening to take. "You mean a great deal to me, too, Warren," she said quickly. "You've always been a good friend to me and my father."

Prescott's mouth quirked in an expression that was half smile, half grimace. "Am I nothing more than a good *friend* to you, Kathy? I always thought—"

"You're a wonderful help to my father," Kathy broke in as if she hadn't heard what he was saying. "I know he wouldn't have been nearly as successful without you."

Prescott stood silently for a long moment, his eyes intently studying the young woman who seemed unwilling or unable to meet his gaze. Then he chuckled ruefully and said, "I'm glad I've always been a good friend."

He went to the door and paused there. Kathy still didn't look up at him.

"Would you like me to send Mary back up here?" he asked.

"No, that's all right. I really can handle the unpacking that's left."

"All right. I'll see you later, Kathy."

Something about his tone said that the situation was not yet resolved, not by a long shot.

Prescott shut the door behind him and then stood in the hall for a moment, shaking his head. Kathy hadn't reacted as he had expected her to, but that didn't mean he was giving up.

He went downstairs to the small bar just off the hotel lobby and ordered a brandy. When the bartender placed the snifter in front of him, he picked it up and carried it to a table in the corner.

The bar was cool and shadowy, and he was the only customer. Prescott sat and sipped his brandy in peace, looking as though he were content with the world. He was proud of his self-control; no one could see the emotions seething inside him.

For many years now there had been an unstated agreement between him and Howell Trainor, evidenced only by occasional hints and innuendoes. That agreement concerned Kathy and her future.

Even as a child she had been beautiful, and Prescott had known that she would grow into a lovely, poised, intelligent woman. From the time she was fourteen, he had been determined that she would someday be his bride. It was true that he was two decades older than Kathy, but that wasn't an insurmountable gap. Most girls married young, and when they married it was to mature men, men who could provide for them and take care of them.

Yes, he was going to marry Kathy when the time came.

When the time came. . . . To Warren Prescott's way of thinking, the time was rapidly approaching. It wasn't too early to start laying some of the groundwork. If everything went according to plan, Howell Trainor's inauguration as governor was only eight months in the future. By that time, Prescott intended to be not only the governor's chief aide but also his son-in-law. He had to smile when he thought about that. After all this time, all the work he had put in, Warren Prescott was going to be a very rich man.

Influence peddling, they called it. Warren Prescott preferred to think of it as a sweet deal, one he had been working toward for fifteen years, ever since he had hooked up with a struggling politician named Howell Trainor.

Prescott had discovered early on that there would always be people willing to repay him for any favors he did them. It had started with him making sure that only certain people got to see Trainor. Others—the ones who didn't cooperate—were turned away. From there, as Trainor began to rely more and more on his aide for advice, Prescott learned that he could sway his employer to vote in such a manner that often someone would feel compelled to show their gratitude. Railroad owners wanted more freedom in the way they ran their lines. Businessmen wanted fewer tariffs on their goods. Bankers wanted protection from the rising grassroots movement that threatened to close down their institutions.

Word got around in the right circles that Prescott could deliver Trainor's vote on either side of almost any issue—for a price. As Trainor's influence in the capitol grew, so did Prescott's private bank account. The "gratuities" he received were always in cash, always delivered by anonymous messengers.

And some of the money always went in Trainor's

account, without the senator's knowledge. Prescott considered it insurance. Trainor had to appear to be equally guilty, if not the actual mastermind of the bribery scheme. That way, should he ever discover what Prescott was doing, he couldn't reveal it without politically cutting his own throat.

It was a tired, dirty, disgusted group of men who reined their horses to a stop in front of the big white house eight miles south of Pecos. The house had three stories. The pitch of the red-shingled roof was steep, and the whitewashed sides glared in the sun. A little shade was provided by some carefully tended trees in the yard.

A veranda ran all the way around the house, and an old man was waiting there for the riders. When they pulled up in front of him, he glared at them and barked, "I see you come back with your tails 'twixt your legs! Where's them cattle those no-good Lindsays stole?"

The spokesman for the group of ranch hands was a wiry man, burned by the sun until his skin looked like old leather. He took off his hat and wiped sweat from the inside of it with a gloved hand.

"We ain't got 'em, boss," he said. "Didn't see hide nor hair of 'em, in fact."

Axel Maddock doubled his bony fists. "Then dammit where are they? They ain't on our range no more, that's for sure."

The leader of the ranch hands slowly shook his head. He didn't want to look at Axel as he said, "I ain't too convinced of that, boss. I figger maybe they just strayed over past the crick. If you recollect, you just sent us off up to Lindsay's and didn't let us look over yonder."

"I recollect," Axel Maddock snapped. "And I still say them blasted Lindsays took 'em. Didn't see 'em nowhere, eh?"

"No, sir. In fact, Jubal and some of the Lindsay hands come up on us and tried to make out like *we* was rustlin' *their* cattle." The man spat next to his horse's hooves. "We threw some lead with 'em, boss."

"Hit any of the sons of bitches?" Axel demanded.

"Don't know for sure. Kind of doubt it."

"And then they ran you back here," Axel said coldly.
A sneer contorted his lined face. "Fine bunch of hands
you are!" He suddenly waved a hand at them. "Go on,
damn you! Get out of my sight!"

The leader looked at his employer for a second and
then wheeled his horse and jerked his head for the men to
follow him. They rode out of the yard, back toward the
bunkhouse. Arguing with the old man wasn't going to
accomplish anything.

Axel Maddock watched them ride off. His features
were set in stern, angry lines, and there was a deep,
abiding bitterness in his watery blue eyes.

In his prime, Axel Maddock had been a powerful,
handsome man. The years and his own bile had robbed
him of much of that, withering him away until he was
nothing but a hulking shadow of what he had once been,
at least physically. His hair and mustache were white, and
his face was lean to the point of gauntness.

But he still ran his ranch, made all the decisions and
issued all the orders. Nobody was going to take that away
from him until he was cold and in the ground.

He walked to one side of the house with the slow,
careful gait of a man who knows his bones are fragile. He
stared hawklike over his territory, the terrain falling gently
away to afford him a view that stretched over quite a few
miles.

Over there on the horizon was the other Maddock
ranch, the one that had belonged to his brother and was
now in the hands of his nephew Evan. Thinking about
Evan put a bad taste in Axel's mouth. He didn't know
where the boy had gone wrong, but he sure as hell didn't
act like a true Maddock!

All of Axel's own sons were gone now, but Evan
might have helped to take their place, if only he hadn't
turned out to be such a weakling. Well, there were still
the two young ones, Johnny and Ted. Ted was just a boy,
but Johnny, now—Axel liked what he had seen of Johnny.

Axel went in the side door of the house, the one that
led into the big kitchen. His wife, Reba, was there, and

two of his daughters-in-law. Axel had trouble thinking of them as relations, though; they were just women who had been married to his sons before the boys had been killed.

The women were preparing supper, cooking in large pots since they had to feed the hands as well as the family. Axel paused, lifted the lid off a stewpot, and sniffed. He replaced the lid and said curtly, "Might do to eat. Those worthless hands didn't get our stock back. They let the Lindsays chase 'em like a pack of dogs. Might as well put up a sign sayin' it's all right for Jubal Lindsay to come on my land and steal from me!"

Axel waited a moment for some kind of response, but none of the three women had anything to say to him. They just went about their work quietly. Snorting, he stamped out of the kitchen, thinking that *no one* had anything good to say today.

He went into his study, a narrow little room in which he always kept the curtains pulled. He liked the dark. The shadows made it easier to go back in his mind to another time, an earlier time, when he ruled this range with an iron hand, by God!

He slammed the study door closed behind him, went to his big rough-hewn desk, and got a bottle of brandy from one of the drawers. In the same drawer he kept a glass, and he poured a generous dollop of the liquor into it.

The smooth brandy made his bones feel a little less brittle. He sipped at it and moved over to a case on the wall where an old rifle was displayed. He put up a hand and touched the fine wood of the Winchester's stock. His life had depended on that rifle more than once.

He was certain that the goddamn Lindsays had started the feud. God, how he hated that family! Old Jubal and his boy Matt were the only ones left, but they had plenty of men to do their dirty work for them. Axel swore, as he had sworn many times in the past, that someday he'd clear the range of the whole dirty lot of them.

He could do it, too . . . if his sons were still alive . . . if he could hire some hands with sand in their craw who didn't turn tail and run as soon as the Lindsays put up a fight . . . if Evan hadn't been such a coward.

Draining the glass, Axel Maddock poured another and settled down to the business of drinking the rest of the afternoon away.

Chapter Four

The next morning found Howell Trainor and Warren Prescott in the Pecos city hall, a sturdy stone building not far from the courthouse. They were meeting with the mayor, who was obviously proud to have them in his office.

"I can't tell you how pleased I am that you gentlemen have come to see me," he said as he sat down behind his desk after ushering them into the room. "Pecos has really been looking forward to your visit, Senator."

"And I've been looking forward to visiting Pecos," Trainor replied with a ready smile.

Though he was still upset about what had happened the previous afternoon, Trainor was a politician above all else. Campaigning was an instinctive thing with him; when he saw an opportunity to garner support, he couldn't help but go after it.

Prescott had arranged this meeting, as he arranged all of Trainor's meetings, but Howell Trainor was in his element here. Prescott was content to sit back and let his employer do what he did best.

"You have a lovely city here," Trainor said, a statement that all three men in the room knew was less than sincere, but one that had to be said. "I noticed a small park in front of the courthouse, complete with a little bandstand."

The mayor leaned forward and smiled knowingly. "A mighty fine place to hold a rally, I'd say."

"Yes, indeed. A band, some nice, stirring patriotic music, perhaps a few speeches."

"My very thoughts, Senator. In fact, I've had posters

put up in the stores around town, announcing that you'll honor us with a few words tonight. I hope that wasn't too presumptuous. . . ."

"Not at all, not at all!" Trainor declared enthusiastically.

Prescott sat there with a smile on his face, not really listening to the conversation between the two men. He had plenty of experience in filtering out the obligatory political chitchat; yet he would still know if Trainor was straying into areas he ought not to discuss. In those cases, an alarm went off in Prescott's head, and he could interject himself into the discussion long enough to steer it back onto safer ground.

But now he was thinking about Kathy Trainor. When he had set out on this journey, he had done so with the intention of becoming engaged to her by the time it was over. So far, however, he had made little progress. His conversation with her the day before in the hotel suite had been his boldest move so far, and it had met with no success. He hadn't pushed it, not wanting to create any sort of tension or strain between them, but his patience would last only so long.

He hoped that it wouldn't come down to having a long, candid talk with Kathy about political realities and expediencies . . . and keeping her father's suspiciously large bank account out of the public eye.

In the meantime, he would wait and see what happened.

While Trainor and Prescott were in the mayor's office conducting their meeting, Kathy had been left to her own devices. After thinking it over, she had decided to see what kind of shopping Pecos had to offer.

Back in Austin, shopping sprees were one of the accepted activities for politicians' daughters, and Kathy had been able to hold her own with any of the other young ladies. It was something to pass the time, and no one looked down on her for participating, as they might have if they had known that she spent another goodly portion of her hours reading the records from the state legislature.

From her early teenage years, Kathy had felt an

intense interest in the political process, in the way society's laws were formulated. It was a fascinating field, she had discovered, but also one totally unsuitable for genteel young ladies. Most people would say the thought of a woman in public office was ludicrous, but Kathy didn't see it that way.

If things ever changed, she was going to be prepared. Until that day came, though, she enjoyed trying on dresses and hats just as much as the next woman.

She walked along the sidewalks of Pecos with Mary Killane at her side, and bringing up the rear a few paces back was Gunther Wagner. Gunther had seen that the man at the livery stable was taking proper care of the stagecoach team, and that was about the extent of his duties during a stop in a town.

Gunther had grumbled considerably about being dragged along on some female shopping trip, but Kathy knew he didn't really mind. She knew he wanted to make sure that none of the locals tried to bother them. He could also carry their purchases, as he was doing now. Gunther had worked for Howell Trainor for eight years, his primary duty consisting of driving the Senator's carriage in the city, and he was devoted to the young woman he had seen growing up in that span of time.

Besides, he got to be around Mary Killane this way. Kathy had been closely observing the interaction between Mary and Gunther for the past few weeks, and despite the coolness with which they spoke to each other and the petty bickering they sometimes engaged in, Kathy was convinced that there were sparks flying between the two of them—and not sparks of hostility, either.

Kathy and the two servants had already visited several dress and millinery shops in Pecos, while Gunther stood near the doors, looking awkward and uncomfortable surrounded by feminine frippery. Now they were on their way to see what else the town had to offer. At the moment, they were passing the entrance of Koehler's Emporium.

A young man came out of the open double doors. He wasn't watching where he was going, but had his head turned to look back over his shoulder as he made a ribald comment to the clerk. He was walking quickly, and Kathy had no chance to avoid him.

The two of them bumped together lightly, hardly more than a brushing of sleeves. Certainly there was no harm done. But the young man stopped in his tracks, as did Kathy, and after a moment in which he regarded her with a slightly stunned look, he swept the flat-crowned black hat from his head and grinned.

"My apologies, ma'am," he said effusively. "Reckon I should watch where I'm goin'."

"That's quite all right," Kathy said. She wanted to move along, away from his intent stare, but he was blocking the sidewalk so that she couldn't pass.

"No, ma'am, it's not all right. I could've hurt you, barrelin' along like that." His grin got wider. " 'Course, even if I'd been lookin', your beauty might've blinded me. No offense, ma'am."

Kathy had to smile slightly. The young man was being forward, but he was handsome, and he had a certain rude charm about him. He wore range clothes, and with his dark hair and mustache, deeply tanned skin, and broad white smile, he cut a dashing figure.

But he also wore a gun in a fancy holster low on his left hip. Kathy wasn't used to dealing with men who wore guns.

"Well, there's no harm done, so . . ." She paused, waiting for him to move aside. He didn't budge, though, just stood there with his hat in his hands, grinning at her.

Mary moved up beside Kathy, a disapproving frown on her face. If the young man was fazed by this united front, he didn't show it.

"I'd like to do something to make up for this little inconvenience, ma'am," he said. "If you'd do me the honor of havin' dinner with me . . ."

"Have dinner with you?" Kathy said indignantly. "I don't even know your name."

"It's Maddock, ma'am. Johnny Maddock."

As soon as the words were out of his mouth, he knew he had made a mistake. Kathy's eyes iced over, and her back stiffened. In a voice as cold as the look she gave him, she said, "If you would be so kind as to step out of the way, sir."

Kathy's father had told her about the Maddock-Lindsay feud, as much as he himself knew. She shared his opinion that the members of both families were roughnecks who considered themselves above the law. Why, it was entirely possible that this young man in front of her had been one of the bunch that nearly wrecked their stagecoach!

Johnny looked puzzled as she glared at him. "I surely didn't mean to offend you, ma'am," he said. "It was just a little bump—"

"This incident is not important, Mr. Maddock," she told him. "The simple fact of the matter is that I consider you and all your kin to be ruffians! Now please step aside."

The attack on his family made Johnny equally angry. He began hotly, "Now see here—"

Suddenly Gunther stepped forward. He had bent down and carefully placed the packages he was carrying on the porch, and now he moved around Kathy and Mary with unusual grace for a man of his size and bulk.

"What's the trouble?" he growled at Johnny.

Johnny looked up at the big bald-headed man towering over him and said, "Who the hell are you?"

"Somebody who doesn't particularly like cowboys, especially ones that bother women," Gunther replied softly. "Now why don't you get out of our way?"

Kathy caught at his arm and said urgently, "I don't want a scene, Gunther. It's all right. Really, it is."

Johnny sized up Gunther and had to admit to himself that he didn't look like anybody to tangle with. He took a slow step back along the sidewalk and lifted his hat to his head.

"I said no offense, ma'am. I meant it."

With that he stepped up onto the first riser of the flight of stairs leading to his brother's office. Kathy and Mary stalked past him rather haughtily. Gunther retrieved the packages and started after the two women, pausing only long enough to grunt, "I'll remember you, cowboy."

"You do that," Johnny snapped back at him.

For a moment, Johnny Maddock watched the trio

move on down the street. Then he started up the stairs toward his brother's office, shaking his head. Sometimes there was no figuring people.

Evan and Billy Chadwell were seated at the table in the big front room when Johnny came into the office. They were wrangling out a tricky legal question, and it was a moment before either of them looked up to see who the visitor was.

When they did, Johnny sauntered into the room and propped a hip on the corner of the table. "Howdy, Evan. Mr. Chadwell."

"Hello, Johnny," Evan replied slowly. "I thought—"

"You thought I was out at the ranch workin'," Johnny finished for his brother. He grinned. "As you can see, I'm right here in town. Got some errands to run."

"What kind of errands?" Evan asked.

"Well . . ." Johnny leaned forward. "Think you could see your way clear to loan me a couple of hundred dollars?"

Evan frowned. "Two hundred dollars? That's a lot of money, Johnny. What's it for?"

"This and that." Johnny shrugged.

"Like a gambling debt?"

Evan's voice was sharp, and Billy Chadwell abruptly stood up and said, "I believe I'll wander on over to the Orient, Evan. Nothing like a few whereases and parties of the second part to give a man a thirst. See you around, Johnny."

Chadwell snagged his hat from the rack and went out of the office. Evan waited until the door was closed behind him before snapping at Johnny, "I hope you know you embarrassed Billy."

Johnny snorted in derision. "Looked to me like it was you doin' the embarrassin', Evan. All I did was ask for a loan."

"Which I'm not going to give you."

Johnny looked as if he wanted to make some sort of angry reply, but then his basically carefree nature took over. He shrugged again and said, "I'll just get it somewhere else."

"You do that." Evan hesitated and then went on,

"You know, all that carousing and gambling you do isn't a very good influence on Ted."

Johnny bristled again. "Maybe not, but if he just had you to go by, he might grow up thinkin' his face would crack if he smiled. There's more to life than workin' and worryin', Evan, even if you don't know it."

Stony faced, Evan watched as Johnny stood up, went to the door, and then paused. After a long moment, Johnny slapped the facing of the door and said, "Ah, hell!" He turned around with a grin. "Never could stay mad at you, Evan."

"I'm glad," Evan said, and meant it.

For all of his wildness, Johnny might have a point, Evan thought. Was there anything to his life except work and worry? He had his happy moments, but they were all tied up with his law practice or with the running of the ranch. How long had it been since he had spent time with his brothers just to enjoy their company? He couldn't remember.

He nodded to the chair that Billy Chadwell had vacated. "Why don't you sit a spell?"

"All right." Johnny reversed the chair and straddled it. "But no lectures, all right?"

"No lectures."

"Good. Maybe you can tell me, Evan, who that pretty little lady was that I nearly ran into downstairs?"

"What pretty little lady?"

Johnny indicated Kathy's height with an outstretched hand. " 'Bout this tall, lots of chestnut hair, shaped nice and trim. Mighty fine lookin' filly."

The description was familiar to Evan. It sounded like Kathleen Trainor. "Was she with anybody?" he asked.

"There was another lady with her, older than her. And some big feller with about as much hair on his head as a cue ball."

That would be Gunther Wagner. Evan sighed and said, "I'll bet she wasn't too friendly when you told her your name." He knew Johnny and the way he was around pretty girls and took it for granted that his brother had introduced himself.

"Not friendly at all. I managed not to get into a fight with her friend, though."

"That was her driver. The other woman was probably her maid. The lady was Kathleen Trainor, Johnny, the daughter of that senator who's visiting here in town."

Johnny let out a whistle. "A senator's daughter, eh? Guess I'm settin' my sights a mite high. But that never stopped me before."

Evan shook his head. "You don't want to mix with that bunch. You could get into trouble real easy there."

Johnny's answering grin was rakish. "Never stopped me before, did it?"

"No. I'm afraid it didn't."

Johnny stood up. "Reckon I can take care of any problems that crop up. I'll just wait till that Gunther feller ain't around."

"Walk careful, Johnny," Evan told him.

Johnny laughed, waved, and slipped out the door.

Billy Chadwell came back into the office a few minutes later. Obviously, he had been waiting for Johnny to leave before returning. As he came in and found Evan staring broodingly down at the table, he said, "Trouble?"

"No more so than usual," Evan said. "Johnny's just feeling his oats. He's got his cap set for the Trainor woman."

Chadwell gave a sigh of acknowledgment. "Oh. That could pose problems, I suppose."

"Damn right it could."

"Well, then, you shouldn't mind coming with me to Trainor's big rally and speechifying tonight."

Evan started to shake his head. "No, thanks, Billy. You know I don't go for all that political hot air."

"You could keep an eye on Kathleen Trainor. Or maybe I should say, you could keep an eye out for Johnny."

Evan nodded thoughtfully. "You have a point there."

"Besides, there's no better lesson for a young lawyer than to watch a high-powered politician in action. Shows you what you might turn out to be if you're not careful."

"All right." Evan chuckled. "You've got me convinced."

But as he and Chadwell went back to work, he couldn't

shake the bothersome feeling that he was letting himself in for more than he had bargained for.

When Evan arrived at the city park that evening, the crowd was sparse but growing. The sun had set, though there was still a rosy glow in the western sky. Lanterns were hung on the posts that supported the circular roof of the bandstand, where the small city band had already assembled.

The day had been another hot one, and not much of the heat had dissipated yet. Ladies and men alike fanned themselves as they settled into their seats on backless wooden benches that faced the bandstand.

Evan spotted Billy Chadwell approaching the park from the opposite direction. They had left the office together, but Chadwell had gone home to the small house he owned on the edge of town, while Evan had returned to the room he rented in Ma Kilgore's boardinghouse, which he used when he wasn't out at his ranch. He had washed up a bit, changed into his churchgoing clothes, and then eaten supper with the other boarders before strolling over to the park.

He and Chadwell met at the rear of the sitting area and found seats about two-thirds of the way toward the front. Chadwell pulled a colorful handkerchief from his pocket and mopped his forehead, then said, "Looks like there might be a pretty good crowd."

"Folks like a show," Evan replied. "Guess they figure Trainor will put on a good one."

"I've been to some of these rallies before. They won't be disappointed."

More people had arrived by now, and the benches were starting to fill up. As Evan continued to chat with Chadwell, he was vaguely aware of someone moving along the bench toward him, stepping past some townspeople seated at the end and then settling down in the empty space to his left.

Evan glanced that way, and he was startled to see Kathy Trainor's equally surprised blue eyes looking back at him. Warren Prescott was seated on her other side.

Obviously, since Evan's head had been averted while he talked to Billy Chadwell, they hadn't noticed who they were about to sit down beside.

Neither Evan nor Kathy said anything to the other. Kathy quickly turned her head and began speaking in a low voice to Prescott. Evan turned his attention forward again, just as Howell Trainor, the mayor, and the town aldermen filed into the park and took seats on the bandstand.

Evan knew from what Johnny had told him earlier that the senator's daughter didn't have any use for the Maddocks, so the coldness he had seen in her eyes didn't surprise him. Once seated, though, she was too proud to get back up and look for somewhere else to sit.

He told himself he didn't care how she felt about him or his family. She was an outsider who didn't know how things really were out here on the frontier.

But he had become something of an outsider himself, he realized. His schooling in Austin and his break with the family tradition of ranching made him different, yet the West was the only real home he had known.

For some reason, Evan's pulse was beating faster than normal. *Must be the heat,* he thought. There was a slight breeze, but it wasn't cooling things off very fast.

He glanced over at Kathy, despite his resolve not to pay any attention to her. She was chatting gaily with Prescott, and as she smiled and laughed, Evan had to admit that her profile was just about perfect.

The Pecos city band usually performed only at the annual rodeo and on major holidays, but it had been gathered together for this occasion, and at a signal from the mayor, it launched into a series of patriotic songs. The music was loud and somewhat mangled, but the stirring rhythms came through anyway. The crowd fell silent, and by the time the mayor stood up to make some opening remarks, the townspeople were in a receptive mood.

"Friends and neighbors, you know why we've all come here tonight. We are honored to have in our fair city one of the state's leading lawmakers, a distinguished senator from our capital city of Austin—and, may I add, quite possibly our next governor! I refer, of course, to the honorable Howell W. Trainor!"

As the audience applauded, Trainor stood up, faced the crowd, and gave a little bow.

The mayor went on for several minutes, describing Trainor's illustrious career in politics. When the crowd started to get a bit restive, the mayor quickly brought his remarks to a close and said, "And now I give you Senator Howell Trainor!"

Nodding and shaking hands briefly with the mayor, Trainor replaced him at the front of the bandstand. Again there was applause, and he waited for it to die down before he started speaking. Evan and Chadwell joined in the applause, but only for the sake of politeness.

"My friends," Trainor began when it was quiet once more, "I want to tell you how very happy I am to be here with you tonight. I've met several of you on an individual basis today, and I want you to know that although I've been all over this great state of ours, nowhere have I encountered such friendly, hospitable people!"

That was hogwash, and Evan knew it. But Trainor's voice was completely sincere as he spoke. Maybe he did really believe what he was saying . . . at least until he reached the next city.

"As you know, Texas is a great state," Trainor went on. "I've seen it all. I've seen the waves of the Gulf washing our shores. I've seen the piney woods of East Texas that seem to go on forever. I've seen the farmlands verdant with crops, the ranchlands and their mighty herds of cattle, the majesty of our mountains here in the west, the starkly barren beauty of our deserts." Trainor held up a clenched fist. "It's a rich land, my friends, and it's *ours!*"

Applause broke out. Trainor waited until it tapered off and then went on, "We fought for this land! Our fathers fought for it! More than likely, our sons will fight for it! Because times are changing, my friends. Texas is no longer alone. We are a state, part of a great, progressive nation that is continually growing. No longer is it enough for a man to have a good horse, a good rifle, a good dog, and a good woman!"

After a dramatic pause, he said, "What you need today is good solid leadership in Austin, someone to protect Texas's interests in an ever-changing society!"

He was a persuasive speaker, Evan thought, and he appeared to be swaying the crowd to his side. They were glad for any kind of entertainment, and Trainor was providing that. Besides, he was eloquent and appeared to be totally sincere. It looked as if he could count on quite a bit of support from Reeves County when it came time to vote in the fall. Several of the local ranchers were on hand, and they could deliver a considerable number of votes through their employees.

Trainor kept talking, and his speech was interrupted more and more often by applause. Evan and Chadwell exchanged looks every time it happened. Neither of them were taken in by what Trainor was saying, but they both recognized the effectiveness of it.

Nearby, Warren Prescott looked at Kathy and saw she was smiling radiantly as she listened to her father's speech. Though she had heard hundreds of variations on it, she never seemed to tire of listening to what he had to say.

The evening was going well, Prescott thought. The senator was saying the things he was supposed to say. Trainor communicated well, you had to give him that.

Suddenly, there was a pounding of hoofbeats. Several riders swept around the corner, coming from the direction of Pecos's red-light district. They were spurring their horses, shouting, and waving their hats in the air. Gunshots rang out.

Women screamed and men cursed as the tightly knit group of riders raced by the park, whooping and shooting. Everyone dived for cover, including Howell Trainor, as bullets clipped through the bandstand roof. None of the shots came close to hitting anyone, though.

Evan and Chadwell both crouched between the benches. A few feet away, Prescott was hovering over a suddenly pale Kathy Trainor. She didn't scream, but she let out a little cry every time one of the guns fired.

Then the riders were past, galloping on down the

street and out of town, still yelling and firing occasionally. Slowly, the crowd in the park got to its feet. They brushed themselves off and glared after the vanishing cowboys; then they began to disperse and head for home.

The mayor frantically tried to brush the dust from Trainor's suit, all the while apologizing. "Drunken lunatics!" he exclaimed. "That's all they were, Senator, just drunken lunatics! Please don't think the city is responsible—"

In a low voice that only the mayor could hear over the babble of the crowd, Trainor hissed, "This is twice in two days that ruffians have disrupted my plans. I think I made a mistake coming here!"

As the mayor tried desperately to reassure him, out in the audience, Kathy Trainor turned to Evan and snapped, "If I wasn't sure of it before, I am now! Your family is no good, Mr. Maddock!"

Evan stared at her, face taut, but made no reply. Instead, Billy Chadwell said angrily, "Here, now! What makes you say that, Miss Trainor?"

Still speaking to Evan, she said coldly, "I saw your brother in that gang of hooligans, Mr. Maddock, and I dare you to deny it!"

Prescott was gently tugging on her arm, not wanting any more of a scene than was necessary, but Evan merely said, "I'm not denying it, Miss Trainor. I saw Johnny, too."

"You did?" Chadwell asked him.

Evan nodded. "Even if I hadn't, I would have known he was involved. This is just the kind of stunt he and his drinking buddies would pull."

"I won't argue with that statement," Kathy said. Then she allowed Prescott to lead her away. She went up to her father and hugged him, trying to console him for having his rally totally ruined.

Evan spoke to Chadwell, though his eyes were still on Kathy. "We might as well go home," he said. "Show's over here."

"I'm afraid you're right," Chadwell sighed. "That was a damn fool stunt for Johnny to pull, Evan. It's not going to make him any friends here in town."

"Not sure he cares about that. He was probably too liquored up to care about much of anything. Well, at least nobody got hurt." Evan paused. "Yet."

"What do you mean by that?"

"I mean," Evan said grimly, "that even though Johnny's twenty years old, I'm going to tan that boy's hide for him next time I see him!"

Chapter Five

Howell Trainor was still fuming as he, Kathy, and Warren Prescott returned to the Trainor suite a quarter of an hour later.

"This Pecos stopover has been nothing but a damned jinx!" he exclaimed as he stalked into the room. "First we're nearly killed by a runaway stage, and then we're almost shot by a bunch of drunken cowboys!"

"I don't think they intended to hurt anyone," Prescott said placatingly, holding his hat in his hands. "They appeared to be just letting off a little steam."

Kathy whirled to face him, her pretty features now suffused with anger. "Letting off a little steam? They were drunk, and they weren't paying the least bit of attention to where their shots were going! I think the whole lot of them should be thrown in jail."

"I couldn't agree more," Trainor snapped. "I intend to see the sheriff again, first thing in the morning."

Prescott repressed a weary sigh. When Trainor was like this, all you could do was let him get the bluff and bluster out of his system—and best that he should do it in private.

Trainor raged for a few moments more and then said firmly, "I think we should leave Pecos in the morning and go on to Fort Stockton. There's no point in staying here."

"I don't know about that, sir," Prescott said, a frown creasing his brow. "These are rough and ready people out here, Senator. If you leave so suddenly, they might think that you were scared by what happened. That wouldn't make a very good impression."

Trainor stared angrily at his side. "Are you calling me a coward?"

"No, sir," Prescott answered hastily. "I know that nothing could be further from the truth. But the people of Pecos don't know you like I do."

That was certainly true, Prescott thought. If the voters knew how easily Howell Trainor could be manipulated and used, they wouldn't even consider casting their ballots for him.

"Well, perhaps you have a point, Warren," Trainor grudgingly admitted, slightly mollified by Prescott's glib dismissal of the incident. "This is still the wild and woolly West, after all, I suppose. We can't have the people thinking that I'm so easily shaken up by a few drunken antics."

"Of course not," Prescott heartily agreed.

Kathy was shaking her head. "I'm still not sure that we should stay. I'm afraid someone is going to get hurt."

Trainor went to her side and put an arm around her shoulders, squeezing reassuringly. "Don't worry, sweetheart," he said. "No one is going to get hurt. But I can't let a bunch of ruffians scare me off. These western counties are important to the campaign."

"East Texas has a great many voters, too," Kathy pointed out.

"The people in East Texas already know who I am. It's the western half of the state that may swing the election."

Kathy forced a smile. "You're right, Dad," she said. She knew perfectly well that arguing with her father about potential voters wasn't going to get her anywhere.

"I'm glad that's settled," Prescott said with a smile. "I have a few private meetings arranged for you, sir, with some of the big ranchers in the area. I'm sure they'll be very interested in the legislation you've proposed that might be to their advantage."

"Interested enough perhaps to make a donation to the campaign?" Trainor asked. He put tonight's debacle out of his mind and turned his thoughts toward salvaging what he could out of this visit to Pecos. There was no point in looking back. A politician had to learn always to look to the future.

"Perhaps that's one of the things you could discuss with them, Senator," Prescott said. He hesitated a moment and then ventured, "I'm glad you didn't decide to cut the trip short, sir. I think a few days' rest will do us all good."

Before Trainor could reply, Kathy sniffed in derision. "I don't see how we are going to get any rest with that feud going on. We're going to be too busy dodging bullets and wild horses."

"Perhaps it won't be that bad," Prescott said with a smile. "I believe I'll leave you alone now, Senator. Good night, Kathy."

"Good night, Warren." She unbent enough from her anger at the Maddocks and Lindsays to give him a quick smile.

With a nod to the senator that Trainor casually acknowledged, Prescott left the room.

Kathy went to the window of the sitting room and pushed back the curtain to look out at the street. At this time of night there was very little traffic; a few pedestrians on the sidewalks and a lone cowboy on horseback were all that she saw. Many of the lights in this section of the city were already out. The Orient Saloon was the center of nighttime activity in this area.

Suddenly, Kathy wished she was back in Austin, back in the friendly confines of the city in which she had grown up. There she didn't have to worry about being caught in the middle of a feud between two groups of hooligans. This was the most extended trip she had ever made away from her home, and everything had gone fairly well until their journey turned west. Then the heat and dust had grown worse, the hardships increasing until they had culminated in this dangerous visit to Pecos.

Trainor came up behind her and rested his hands on her shoulders. His head was full of thoughts about the meetings set up by Prescott, but he could tell that something else was bothering his daughter.

"It's not that bad, Kathy," he said softly. "We'll only be here a few more days, and then we'll be moving on."

"To some other city as wild as this one?" Kathy reached up and patted her father's hand. "Don't worry about me, Dad. I guess I'm just a little homesick."

"I know. I'm sure everything will be fine. After all, Warren thinks we should stay, and you know what good advice I've gotten from Warren over the years."

Kathy nodded. Warren Prescott had been a help to her father, that was true enough, but even he could make mistakes. He had made one the day before when he started talking about how much he cared for her. Kathy hadn't expected him ever to get any romantic notions about her. Why, he was almost old enough to be her father. He had surprised her with his talk, and she was afraid she hadn't reacted very well. She hoped she hadn't offended him. So far, there was no indication that she had.

In the room across the hall from the suite, Warren Prescott was also wrestling with a problem.

Until the incident outside of Pecos, the trip had gone very well, he thought. Trainor's name was becoming more well known, and that was the key to winning an election. And once the election was won, Prescott could get on about his real business: lining his pockets with as much money as he could rake off.

With Trainor in the governor's mansion, the setup would be perfect. As chief executive, Trainor could throw the weight of his office behind the proposed antitariff bill. Then there was the Hawkes County reservoir deal, the Railroad Commission legislation, the investigation into the banking industry by Senator Winfield's committee . . .

If the antitariff bill and the reservoir act were pushed through, if the Railroad Commission were killed, if the results of Winfield's snooping were quashed, then Prescott stood to gain at least fifty thousand dollars from grateful principals. And that was just the beginning.

He wasn't going to let a few setbacks ruin his plans.

Maybe they *should* leave Pecos, he thought as he fired up a cigar and then took a flask of brandy from his luggage. There weren't *that* many votes to be gained in a jerkwater city like this one. Since Trainor was in danger of losing his composure and making a fool of himself, perhaps it would be best to move on.

Prescott had a hunch that they should stay, though. There would be plenty of times in the future, especially if Trainor won the election, when circumstances would be adverse and the easiest thing might be to back out.

Maybe this was a test, Prescott decided as he sipped the smooth liquor from the flask. Maybe Pecos had been put in Trainor's path as a stumbling block, just to see how he could handle a problem.

And there was something else, some gut instinct that told Prescott something was to be gained in this bustling young city, an opportunity just waiting to be seized.

He recapped the flask, replaced it in his luggage, and then blew out the lamp on the dressing table. He went to the window and looked out at the night. He was feeling a more urgent concern than concern about the future of his employer's career. The thought of undressing and going to bed occurred to him, but he knew he would never be able to sleep, not with the pressures that were bearing down on him. He needed some sort of release.

Warren Prescott knew that Pecos was no different from any of the other cities they had visited on this journey. There was always a place where a man could go for release, for relaxation.

And he needed something stronger than brandy. He needed a woman.

A few discreet inquiries of one of the hotel clerks had already told him where Pecos's red-light district was to be found. Now he settled his hat back on his head and slipped into the hall. He paused at the door of the Trainor suite and listened for a moment; he heard nothing coming from within. Trainor and Kathy had probably already retired for the night.

With any luck, Warren Prescott mused, the night was just beginning for him.

The night was still young, but already the young woman called Celestina was tired. She moved from table to table in the Flores Cantina, carrying drinks to the cowboys who talked and laughed loudly as they played their card games.

Sometimes when she set the glasses and bottles on the tables, one of the men would reach up and caress her breast or run his dirty hand along her hip and thigh. But always she simply smiled, nothing more, no matter how much revulsion she felt inside.

She knew quite well that if one of these cowboys wanted her enough to pay fat Ramirio Flores behind the bar, she would have to go with him to the shacks behind the cantina. That's what the filthy little hovels were there for.

When you came right down to it, that was the only real reason for her existence, too: to be a servant and a plaything for any man with the money to buy her.

Thank goodness for Cal, she thought as she glanced at the man sitting alone at the table in the corner. He was different. He never treated her as if she were a piece of goods to be bought and sold.

She placed a bottle of mescal on the scarred surface of a table where three cowboys were singing a bawdy Spanish song, neatly avoided the groping hand of one of them, and made her way to the table where Cal Ahern sat. Flores had just ducked into the back room, and she thought she could snatch a moment with her lover before the cantina's proprietor reappeared.

Ahern lifted his eyes from the table as the beautiful young woman reached over and slipped her hand into his. He smiled crookedly at her, his eyes slighty bleary from the whiskey he had consumed during the evening.

Celestina was so lovely, he thought. Her long raven hair hung down her back like flowing silk, and her dark eyes flashed with hot inner fires as she gazed at him. With her lithe figure and her smooth brown skin, she was like some beautiful animal, wild and free.

And she was deeply in love with him, Ahern knew. At least, she thought she was. She loved his practiced charm, his facade of culture and sophistication. But then it didn't take much to impress a Mexican whore in a place like Pecos.

Ahern was only twenty-eight years old, but he looked a good ten years older than that. He had been on his own since the age of twelve, when he had run away from a cruel father and an indifferent mother back in Georgia. Somehow he had wound up on a riverboat plying the Mississippi, working for his passage as a cabin boy. Also traveling on the same boat was a man named Yancy, and Ahern had found himself making friends with the man.

Yancy made his living at the gambling tables in the plush salons of the boat. It didn't take long for both of them to realize that Ahern had the talents necessary to follow in Yancy's footsteps. He was quick of hand and eye, and he could deal from the bottom of the deck without ever showing a hint of nervousness on his face.

Yancy was long dead now. His fingers had slipped at just the wrong moment—the only time in years, if he had been telling the boy the truth—and a red-faced horse breeder from Tennessee had shot him for trying to palm an ace. Ahern had evened the score himself two nights later, finding the horse breeder taking a stroll along the shadowy section of the deck. Two quick thrusts of a knife had finished him off, and then Ahern slipped over the side and swam to shore. One stolen horse later, he was on his way west, armed only with his wits and the skills that Yancy had taught him.

So far, that had been enough.

Now he wore an expensive suit and a pearl-gray Stetson. The suit was starting to show a bit of wear, but it was still nicer than anything else to be found in the cantina. A small, well-oiled revolver rode in a cross-draw holster underneath the coat, and there was also a derringer cleverly concealed up his right sleeve. His boots were polished to a glossy sheen. Judging from his appearance, no one would guess that the gambler was nearly flat broke.

Pecos just hadn't been profitable at all. He had wandered into this city, and it looked as if it was just about time to wander back out again.

Celestina was so devoted to him, though, so eager and willing. And Flores gave him a break on the liquor he consumed. Ahern was a better class of customer than the cantina usually attracted, and he figured that Flores hoped his presence would be a draw for more and better-paying patrons.

Besides, there were still people in this city who owed him money . . . like Johnny Maddock.

"You are troubled, Cal?" Celestina said softly as she leaned forward to study his face. It was a handsome face, even when it was frowning. To her way of thinking, Cal did not take care of himself properly, did not eat enough, and that showed up in the lean lines of his features, but he was still the most attractive man she had ever seen.

He kept himself clean; that alone was enough to lift him above the cowhands and vaqueros who frequented this place.

Ahern squeezed her hand. "It is nothing, *querida,*" he said. "Don't concern yourself."

"I get you something to eat, yes?"

"You get me something to eat, no. But you can bring over another bottle when you get the chance."

"Cal, you drink too much," she sighed. "I know it is not my place to tell you this, but I worry about you."

Ahern's face went taut, and he slowly disengaged his fingers from hers.

"You're not my mama, Celestina," he said stiffly. "Don't try to act like it. Act like my woman instead."

Celestina dropped her eyes, chastened by his words. "*Sí,*" she whispered, dropping her hand beneath the table to run it along his leg. "I am your woman, Cal. I will not forget again."

Ahern took a deep breath and willed himself to relax, willed the sudden anger and tension he had felt to go away. The woman had meant no harm, and she was so desperately eager for his forgiveness. He felt a pang of guilt for speaking so sharply to her.

"It's all right," he said awkwardly. "Don't worry about it."

"*Sí.*" She looked up at him again, and now her face broke into a radiant smile. "I see you later, all right?"

"Sure." Ahern nodded. He knew she wanted to get

back to work before Flores emerged from the back room.
"You go on now."

She got up from the table and started to turn away,
and as she did go, Ahern fetched her an affectionate slap
on her shapely rump. She threw him another smile and
danced away toward the bar.

Celestina was happy again. As long as she had Cal,
she could ignore all the sordid burdens she was forced to
endure. All the other men meant nothing, so long as Cal
showed her affection. And maybe someday—just maybe—he
would take her away from all this.

At first, in her brief moment of euphoria, she didn't
even notice the other man who entered the cantina wearing fine clothes, more expensive clothes than Cal Ahern's.
But then Ramirio Flores came out of the back room,
caught Celestina's eye, and nodded curtly toward the table in the rear of the room where the stranger sat.

Celestina sighed and turned toward the table. She
walked over to it, hips swaying.

Warren Prescott watched her making her way toward
him, and his lips quirked slightly in an appreciative smile.
The hotel clerk had told him that some of the prettiest
women in town were to be found at the Flores Cantina,
and judging by the one coming to take his order, the man
hadn't been exaggerating.

"May I help you, señor?" the young woman asked
huskily as she paused beside the table. She leaned forward
slightly so that the low-cut bodice of her white linen
blouse gave him an unrestricted view of the swells of her
breasts.

"Tequila," Prescott told her with a smile that she
returned. He could tell it was a whore's smile, with no
real feeling behind it, but he didn't particularly care.

"Sí, señor. Un momento."

She glided away, back to the bar, and Prescott enjoyed that as much as he had enjoyed watching her come
toward him. She returned a minute later carrying a wooden
tray that bore a glass and a bottle of tequila. At least he
assumed that the almost clear liquid was tequila; there was
no label on the bottle.

Prescott reached into his pocket and flipped a coin to her. She snatched it deftly out of the air and paused briefly, as though resisting the temptation to bite it and check its authenticity.

Prescott thought about asking her to join him, but then decided it was too soon. He wanted a few drinks first. Alcohol always helped to loosen the tight rein he had to keep on himself most of the time.

He poured a drink as she went away, tasted the liquor, licking his lips. The tequila was raw and burned going down, but a delicious warmth was already spreading in his stomach.

For the next fifteen minutes, he sat there by himself, sipping the fiery tequila and watching the cantina's patrons come and go. Twice, cowboys came into the place through a rear door, their arms around pretty Mexican waitresses, and Prescott guessed correctly that there were cribs out back where the girls could ply their other trade. Several other bar girls were working in the cantina; probably any of them could be had for the proper price, paid in advance no doubt to the sweating, balding, mustachioed little man behind the bar.

Funny thing, though. The woman who had brought him his drink was easily the most attractive one in the room, yet in the time he had been here, no one had approached her to go back to the cribs.

Perhaps that had something to do with the man sitting in the corner, the one wearing a once-elegant suit and a slightly battered pearl-gray Stetson. Prescott noticed that the woman frequently dropped by the table to say a brief word to the man in the Stetson. Once she even sat down with him for a moment, and their hands intertwined on the table.

Ah, romance, Prescott thought cynically. The man had the look of a down-at-heels gambler, and the woman was nothing more than a common saloon slut, but the two of them were in love. At least the woman was. Adoration was plain on her face when she looked at the gambler.

Well, there were other girls, Prescott decided with a mental shake of his head. He wanted to accomplish what he had come here for with no fuss or fanfare. The last thing he needed was to get involved in a shooting or a knifing over a woman like that.

As Prescott was looking around the cantina, trying to settle on which one of the women he preferred, another newcomer pushed through the swinging doors of the entrance.

Prescott felt a momentary surge of recognition as his eyes fell on the man who had just come into the cantina. Then he realized that he had never seen the man before but was reminded by him of someone else—Evan Maddock.

Though he had never met Johnny Maddock, Prescott had no doubt that he was looking at Evan's younger brother. The family resemblance was strong. There was a reckless grin on Johnny's face, though, something that Prescott could not imagine of attorney Evan Maddock.

And there was a Colt riding on Johnny's hip, too, another notable difference.

Johnny sauntered cockily to the bar, as if he was well aware that several pairs of eyes in this room were following him. Over an hour had passed since he and his friends had disrupted Trainor's speech. Evidently he figured that the uproar over that stunt would have subsided by now That conclusion seemed to be correct. No one confronted him about it as he went to the bar.

Putting his hands flat on the crudely constructed bar, Johnny grinned at Ramirio Flores and said, "Tequila, amigo. And leave the bottle."

Flores put bottle and glass on the bar and let Johnny pour his own drink. Johnny filled the glass, tossed down the liquor, and then tipped the bottle up for a refill. He swayed slightly as he did so, enough to show that he was still drunk from earlier in the evening.

At the rate he was drinking, Prescott thought, he was going to be a lot drunker before the night was over.

Prescott was hardly the only one watching Johnny Maddock, he realized. Several of the men in the cantina had been at Trainor's rally, and they probably knew that Johnny had been involved in the commotion that ended it.

The man at the corner table was watching him, too, his eyes narrowed to slits.

Johnny leaned on the bar now, supporting himself on one elbow while he used the other hand to lift the glass to his mouth.

If he continued at this rate, Prescott thought, he'd be passed out on the floor in a little while.

A movement from the corner caught Prescott's eye, and he turned his head to watch the gambler shove his chair back and stand up. There was a strange, intent look on the man's face.

Cal Ahern was glad to see Johnny Maddock enter the cantina, though he didn't like the boy. Johnny Maddock was a regular customer, and he liked to gamble. He just wasn't very good at it, and as a result he owed money to Ahern. A goodly sum, in fact, enough to stake him, enough to let him leave this city with more than the shirt on his back. Ahern took a deep breath and then started toward the bar to collect his money.

Celestina took a step forward as she saw Ahern start toward Johnny Maddock, but he caught her eye and shook his head. She halted, unwilling to go against his wishes.

Ahern stopped behind Johnny and said in a clear voice, "Where's that two hundred you owe me, Maddock?"

Johnny paused in his drinking, the glass—once again filled with tequila—halfway to his mouth. Without tasting the liquor, Johnny slowly replaced the glass on the bar and swung half around to see who was accosting him.

"Well, howdy there, Cal," he said with a mocking grin. "What was that you said?"

"You owe me two hundred dollars," Ahern replied flatly. "I want it."

Johnny straightened and turned all the way around, facing Ahern and putting his back to the bar. The grin was still plastered on his face, but his eyes had gone hard and cold.

"I told you I'd get the money to you," he said, "but I haven't gotten it yet. Reckon you'll just have to wait."

Ahern shook his head. "I'm tired of waiting. Damn tired."

"That's too bad," Johnny said with a mirthless chuckle. "Don't know what I can do about it, though."

Ahern felt his temper slipping away from him. He tried to bring it under control, but to no avail.

Johnny started to turn away from the gambler, back to the bar. Ahern reached out and grabbed his arm. "You cheap, no-good welsher!" Ahern spat.

Moving quicker than Ahern had expected, Johnny spun around. He threw Ahern's grip off his arm and took a quick step backward. A vile epithet burst from his mouth as he glared at the gambler.

"Cal, no!" Celestina cried as she saw Ahern start to reach for the gun underneath his coat.

Johnny Maddock's hand flickered down to his hip, instinct and practice coming together to produce a blindingly fast draw.

Before Ahern could even come close to pulling his gun from his holster, he was staring down the menacing black barrel of Johnny's Colt.

"I told you you'd have to wait," Johnny said icily, "and I meant it."

Ahern could feel his pulse thundering in his head as he looked into the yawning muzzle of the pistol. Drunk or not, Johnny's hand was steady, and the gun didn't waver. After spending years figuring odds, Ahern knew this was one situation he couldn't buck.

"Take it easy, Maddock," he said quietly. "I don't want any trouble."

"Then don't go looking for any," Johnny warned him. "I'll pay you that money as soon as I can. Until then, steer clear of me, understand?"

"Sure, Johnny. I understand."

Slowly, Ahern backed away from Johnny Maddock. The younger man waited a moment and then holstered the Colt, but he kept his eye on the gambler until Ahern was back at his corner table. If Ahern tried any tricks, Johnny was ready.

Fighting the fear and contempt that flooded through him, Ahern sat down at the table and reached for the bottle of whiskey. The contempt was for himself—once more he had backed down from a fight. It seemed he always took the easy way out, no matter how determined he was to stand up for himself.

He was a coward, plain and simple, he thought. And he hated Johnny Maddock for knowing that as well as he himself did.

Ahern didn't bother with the glass this time. He tipped the bottle up and drank directly from it.

Warren Prescott had watched the episode between Ahern and Johnny Maddock with a faint smile on his face. The gambler didn't have the stomach for violence, that was obvious. That kind of man rarely did, Prescott thought. It took a special breed of man to go after what he wanted and damn any obstacles in his path. A man like himself . . .

" . . . don't know why you let no-accounts like that gambler hang around here," Johnny was saying to Flores. Diplomatically, Flores said nothing in return as Johnny continued to make disparaging comments about Ahern, his voice loud enough to be plainly audible all through the room. Ahern seemed to be ignoring him, though.

A man stepped out of the shadows of the cantina's rear entrance. Lagging a few feet behind him was one of the bar girls, and from her disheveled state it was obvious that the two of them were returning from one of the shacks out back.

Conversation in the cantina had fallen off during the confrontation between Johnny and Ahern, but now it was building back up again. As the newcomer spoke up, silence dropped over the room like a falling curtain.

"Always heard you was fast with a gun, Johnny," the man said. "That draw of yours was mighty nice, but why don't we see how you stack up against somebody you can't buffalo?"

Carefully, Johnny turned away from the bar again, responding to this challenge. A cold grin stretched over his face when he saw who had spoken.

"Howdy, Lindsay," Johnny said lazily. "You got something to say to me?"

"Just said it," Matt Lindsay replied. "Let's see who's the fastest, you or me."

"Sounds like a fine idea." Johnny stepped away from the bar, his hand hanging close to the butt of his gun.

Warren Prescott leaned forward to watch more closely. The infamous Maddock-Lindsay feud was unfolding right in front of him in miniature, and he found himself fascinated. The feeling of hatred in the room was almost a physical thing.

Chairs scraped hurriedly as the cantina's other customers got out of the way.

Johnny and Matt were facing each other about ten feet apart, both of them ready to draw. They were both still grinning, but their eyes told a different story. This was a deadly business for them.

Before either of them could make another move, Ramirio Flores stepped out from behind the bar and leveled a double-barreled shotgun at them.

"No shooting in here," he snapped, the shotgun backing up his command. "I never got paid for the broken bottles the last time two hotheads decided on a little gunplay."

Flores was behind Matt but standing at such an angle that a blast from the shotgun would hit both of the young men. Matt shot a glance over his shoulder and said nervously, "Dammit, Flores, put that thing up! I've heard tell it's got a hair trigger."

"You heard tell right, amigo."

Johnny took a deep breath. His drunkenness seemed to have vanished, and other than a red face, Matt Lindsay wasn't showing any signs of being intoxicated either.

"There'll be another time, Matt," Johnny said.

Matt Lindsay licked dry lips. "Yeah," he said tonelessly. "Another time."

Prescott thought that both of the young men looked mighty relieved that Flores had given them an excuse to call off the gunfight before it began. They could have moved their showdown to the street, but neither of them mentioned that possibility.

They were hotheaded and proud, all right, but neither wanted to die.

Matt Lindsay suddenly spat into the sawdust on the

floor. "The class of people drinkin' here sure has gone downhill," he said with a bitter little laugh. "Reckon I'll get on over to the Double Eagle. They know how to treat a man there."

He squared his shoulders and stalked out of the cantina, not looking back. He knew Johnny wasn't going to shoot him from behind.

As soon as Matt disappeared through the swinging doors, Johnny turned to the bar and slapped his palm down on it. He glared at Flores, who was lowering the shotgun.

"What's a man have to do to get some service around here?" Johnny demanded.

Flores replaced the shotgun on the shelf underneath the bar as he hurried to bring a fresh bottle to Johnny. The place had been dead quiet during the moment when Matt and Johnny had faced each other; now the sound of voices began to pick up again. There were jokes and laughter as the interrupted card games resumed.

The wheels of Warren Prescott's mind were starting to turn. They picked up speed as he looked into the corner and saw the pure hatred with which the gambler Ahern regarded Johnny Maddock.

Over the years, Prescott had learned to be on the lookout for anything that might further the career of Howell Trainor. Every rung of the political ladder that Trainor climbed meant another step up for Prescott as well, another step toward his ultimate goal of wealth and power. After watching the clash between Maddock and Lindsay, he had the glimmerings of an idea.

Prescott caught Celestina's eye and signaled for her to come over to the table. The tension of the last few minutes had shaken her somewhat, and the calculated erotic appeal was gone from her walk as she approached him. That still left her own natural sensuousness, though, a quality that Prescott could have appreciated under other circumstances. Right now he had other things on his mind.

"What can I bring you, señor?" Celestina asked as she approached.

Prescott waved a hand at the bottle of tequila sitting

on the table. It was still half full. "Nothing to drink," he said.

Celestina sighed and looked at the back door, as though seeing beyond it to the cribs. "You wish something else?"

"That's right," Prescott told her. "I want you to ask your friend to come over here. I want to talk to him."

Celestina frowned in confusion. "My friend? I do not understand, señor."

Prescott looked pointedly at Ahern. "The man over there in the corner," he said. "Ask him to come over."

Celestina nodded, not knowing what this fancy-dressed American wanted with Cal. She went over to the corner table and spoke briefly to the gambler.

Prescott saw Ahern look up at him, the puzzlement on his face mirroring Celestina's. But then Ahern shoved his chair back, stood up, and made his way across the room.

"Something I can do for you, friend?" he asked as he came to a stop beside Prescott's table.

Prescott waved a hand at the vacant chair across the table and said, "Sit down, Mr. . . . Ahern, is it?"

"That's right." Still frowning, Ahern slowly sat down. Prescott offered him a drink of the tequila, but Ahern shook his head. "What's this about?"

Prescott looked toward the bar, and Ahern followed his gaze. The exhilaration of facing death had momentarily sobered Johnny Maddock, but as he leaned on the bar, he was rapidly getting back to his original drunken state. He was talking loudly to Flores, laughing at his own jokes.

"Seems to be a lot of hot blood in this town," Prescott said.

Ahern grunted. "A lot of loudmouthed bastards, if you ask me."

"Young Maddock there seems to be the kind of man who makes a great many enemies." A conspiratorial smile creased Prescott's face as he leaned forward. "I have a proposition that may prove to be very interesting for you, Mr. Ahern. . . ."

Chapter Six

It's a damn good thing that the horse knows the way home, Johnny Maddock thought fuzzily, *because I sure as blazes don't*.

He rode easily, swaying only slightly in the saddle, not appearing nearly as drunk as he really was. Years spent on horseback were responsible for that. He was more at home riding than he was on his feet, and the past few years he had had quite a bit of experience at staying in the saddle when he'd had too much to drink, as well.

It was late, very late. A slice of moon hung low in the sky. The stars were still shining brightly, though, casting enough of a glow for Johnny to see the road that led through the chaparral from Pecos to the ranch.

Several hours had passed since the encounter with Matt Lindsay at the Flores Cantina. The business with Ahern that had preceded it had already slipped from Johnny's mind, but the memory of the near-gunfight with Matt was still crystal clear.

Matt had been drinking, too, Johnny knew, but that didn't really matter. He was still fast.

As fast as Johnny himself? Johnny didn't know, and for the moment he wouldn't be finding out.

He had been scared. He didn't mind admitting that to himself, even though he wouldn't have said as much to anyone else. There was nothing wrong with a little good healthy caution when you were facing down another man with a gun. The thought that you might be the one to die kept a good sharp edge on you that might not be there otherwise.

That was an edge he had to keep, Johnny thought,

76

because it looked as if there might be a lot of shooting in the near future. He had heard about the clash between Axel Maddock's hands and the Lindsay riders a couple of days earlier. The feud seemed to be heating up again, which was just fine with Johnny.

It made him ashamed to think about it, but here he was, twenty years old and he had yet to swap bullets with any of the Lindsays. Things had been kind of quiet the last few years, with only an occasional clash now and then, and the opportunity to spill some Lindsay blood had never come up until tonight.

As fast as he was with a gun, Johnny Maddock had never killed a man.

That was going to change, though, he was sure of it. The honor of the Maddocks had to be upheld, and he was just the man to do it. He'd show Uncle Axel that not all of the men on his side of the family were spineless cowards. Like Evan . . .

The thought of Evan made Johnny even more melancholy as he rocked along in the saddle. It was a hard thing, being unable to respect your older brother. Oh, Evan was smart enough, all right, but he devoted all of his energies to that damned law practice instead of concentrating on the important things—like settling the score with the bastards responsible for the deaths of their father and brothers.

Evan was yellow. That was the only explanation that made any sense, hard as that was for Johnny to swallow.

The sound of hoofbeats in the night brought him out of his reverie.

Johnny pulled rein on his horse, softly saying, "Whoa, boy." He twisted in the saddle and peered back at the trail behind him. Someone was coming up at a pretty good clip.

Could Matt Lindsay have followed him out here to continue their fight?

Johnny turned his horse's head and prodded him off the road, forcing his way into the dense undergrowth to the side. Whether the approaching rider was Matt Lindsay or someone else, Johnny didn't want to face him. Chances were the man meant him no harm, but he was too drunk right now to risk any trouble—and smart enough to know it.

Johnny sat his horse silently, several yards off the road, and waited for the other rider to pass. He couldn't see anything through the thick chaparral, but the sound of the horse's hooves was loud in the night.

The hoofbeats stopped, and Johnny knew then that the man had seen him leave the road. Nights out here on the plains were cold, but Johnny felt a chill go through him that had nothing to do with the weather.

All his instincts told him this was trouble.

He put his hand on his gun as the other rider suddenly loomed up in front of him, a deeper patch of darkness in the shadows. His heart pounding, Johnny called out, "Hold it right there, friend," and started to slip his Colt out of its holster.

He saw movement in the shadows and suddenly knew that he was too late. His drunken condition had slowed him down just enough.

Noise and flame blasted out of the darkness. Johnny felt something slam into his chest, and then he was falling. His pistol had barely cleared his holster, and it slipped from his fingers as he crashed to the ground. He had the presence of mind to kick his feet free of the stirrups, so the horse couldn't drag him if it bolted, but then the fire coursing through him blotted out everything else. His fingers scrabbled weakly in the sand, and he tried to lift his head so that he could see the man who had shot him.

He didn't make it. His face fell forward, sand and grit filling his mouth and nose. But he didn't feel it.

For Johnny Maddock, the feud was over.

The next morning dawned bright, clear, and hot, as usual, in Pecos. Evan Maddock was in the law office early, going over Chadwell's law books in search of a precedent for a case they were preparing. He became so absorbed in the work, as he often did, that he lost track of time until Billy Chadwell came breezing into the room. Chadwell's arrival meant that it was midmorning, at least.

"Morning, morning," Chadwell said as he hung his

hat on the peg inside the door. "Why is it you always beat me to the office, Evan?"

"Age has its privileges," Evan replied dryly. "I suppose sleeping late is one of them."

Chadwell chuckled. "That'll teach me to ask foolish questions," the old lawyer said. "What are you working on?"

"Thought I'd start laying the groundwork for the Baxter case. It'll be coming up before you know it."

"True enough." Chadwell pulled out a chair on the other side of the table and sat down. His face became serious as he went on, "Evan, have you heard any talk around town about what happened last night in the Flores Cantina?"

Evan looked up in surprise. "The cantina? I haven't heard anything about it. What happened, another shooting?" Evan knew that violence was a common occurrence in that part of town.

"There was no shooting, but it was a close thing. Two men almost went for their guns." Chadwell paused and then went on, "Johnny was one of them, Evan. He and Matt Lindsay almost drew on each other."

Evan was holding a pen, which he had been dipping in an inkwell to make notes as he studied the books. Now he slowly laid the pen on the table and stared at Billy Chadwell. His face was grim, and after a moment he softly said, "Damn."

"It could have been worse, Evan," Chadwell hastily added. "At least neither of them was hurt."

Evan rose to his feet and strode over to the window. "I was afraid something like this would happen," he said over his shoulder. "When I heard about that business the other day between the Lindsays and Uncle Axel's men, I knew the feud was starting up again. It's been too quiet for too long."

"They're both young, and they're both hotheaded and proud. It doesn't have to amount to anything. Just have a talk with Johnny—"

"He won't listen to me. He never has."

Chadwell spread his hands helplessly. "I'd talk to the

boy myself, but you know he and I have never been close. Not like you and me, anyway."

Evan was pacing back and forth in front of the windows. He shook his head. "Won't do any good to talk to him. I don't think there's any way through that hard head of his. I've seen mules you could reason with better."

Chadwell smiled. "Maybe so. I'm just glad we don't have a killing to contend with. Leaving out the fact that Johnny's your brother, if they had shot it out the whole town would be just about ready to explode. I don't want to see a war in Pecos."

"Neither do I, Billy, neither do I." Evan came back to the table and sat down. "There's nothing we can do about it now. What say we get back to work?"

"Sounds like a good idea to me," Chadwell agreed.

The two of them fell to their task, hashing out the details of the upcoming case, and once again Evan was able to lose himself in the work. A nagging worry about Johnny never totally left his thoughts these days, but at least while he was concentrating on something else he was able to shove the damned feud to the back of his mind.

They had been working for about half an hour when the door of the office opened. Evan looked up and frowned in surprise when he saw that the visitor was Warren Prescott.

Billy Chadwell turned around in his chair and also recognized Prescott. If he was as puzzled as Evan, though, he didn't show it. He simply said, "Well, good morning, Mr. Prescott. What can we do for you?"

Prescott took off his hat. He was his usual well-groomed self this morning. He said, "I've come to ask a favor, gentlemen."

"Glad to oblige. What can we do for the senator?" As he spoke, Chadwell waved for Prescott to have a seat at the table.

Prescott pulled back a chair and sank into it, placing his hat on the table. "Actually, Mr. Maddock here is the one who can do me the favor," he said, leaning forward with a smile.

"Me?" Evan asked. "I'm not sure what I can do for you, Mr. Prescott."

"You know the area well, don't you?"

"Why, Evan knows every trail in the county," Chadwell said before Evan could reply.

"And I know a young attorney like yourself has his finger on the pulse of the community," Prescott continued.

Evan's instinct told him to be wary. "Reckon I keep up with things pretty well," he said slowly.

"Then you're just the man I need. I want to pick your brain, Mr. Maddock. Figuratively speaking, of course." Prescott got to his feet and started to walk around the office, thumbs hooked in his vest. Evidently he was more comfortable moving around. "You see, the senator relies on me for a great deal of information regarding the political climate. I've found that the best way to obtain that information is to go right to a well-informed citizen and discuss things with him. I need to get the true facts of a situation, and if I talked only to elected officials, I'd only hear things that made them look good."

"Folks do tend to paint things the colors they like," Chadwell said.

"Exactly," Prescott agreed. "But a man like you has no vested interests, Maddock. If I read you right, the main thing you're interested in is making Pecos and the surrounding country a better place to live. Am I right?"

"I'd like to see the city grow and prosper," Evan admitted. "If you want to ask me some questions, go ahead. I'll answer them as best I can. But the man you really ought to talk to is sitting right here." He nodded at Chadwell.

Chadwell shook his head. "No, Mr. Prescott's right," he said. "He's too polite to say it, but my time has about run its course, Evan. Oh, I plan on being around a long time yet, but it's you young folks who have to determine what the future's going to be like."

"I guess I can see that." Evan shrugged his shoulders. "Ask away," he said to Prescott.

Prescott hesitated. "Well, you see there's another

favor I have to ask of you, and I'd like to combine the two if I could."

Again, Evan felt the urge to be cautious. "What might this other favor be?"

"Miss Trainor has decided that she'd like to take a ride around the countryside. She's an excellent rider, you know."

"No. I didn't know that," Evan said.

The truth of the matter was, there were a great many things he didn't know about Kathy Trainor, and he didn't figure he'd ever get a chance to find them out.

"Oh, yes, she's been riding since she was a little girl. She asked me to accompany her this morning, but I'm afraid I would probably lose our way quite rapidly once we got out of sight of town. So I thought perhaps the three of us . . ."

Evan shook his head in disbelief, remembering the disdain on Kathy's face when she looked at him, the anger and scorn in her voice as she had lashed him with her harsh words.

"I don't think Miss Trainor would like to go riding with me," he said.

"She was a bit surprised when I suggested that you go with us," Prescott admitted. "But she's not a young lady who holds a grudge. Anyway, you've never done anything to make her dislike you. We can't hold a person responsible for what the rest of his family does. I told that to the senator, as well as to Miss Kathy. I want to apologize to you on their behalf for some of the things they've said to you."

Evan waved that off. "No apology necessary," he said. "People say things when they're upset." He gestured at the law books and notes spread out on the table. "I'm afraid I'll have to pass on your invitation, though. I've got too much work to do this morning."

Billy Chadwell spoke up. "Don't worry about the work, Evan," he said. "I think you should go with Miss Trainor and Mr. Prescott."

Evan glanced at his partner in surprise. "You do?"

"I certainly do. I think you could be a great help to

Mr. Prescott; you know as much about the political situation around here as anybody, and you're objective. And I'm sure Miss Trainor would enjoy having you along to point out some of the interesting sights in the area."

"Well, what about it, Mr. Maddock?" Prescott asked.

Evan glanced again at Billy Chadwell, who nodded. "All right," Evan said. "Looks like you've got yourself a guide, Mr. Prescott. Hope I live up to your expectations."

"I'm sure you will. And how about calling me Warren?"

Evan nodded and reached for his hat and rifle. Anyone who rode much on the range carried a rifle, if for no other reason than to protect against snakes. "All right, Warren. I'm ready. See you later, Billy."

"Don't hurry," Chadwell said, grinning. "Thanks for getting this young fella out of the office, Mr. Prescott."

Chadwell watched the two men leave the office, and the grin dropped from his face as the door closed behind them.

Prescott was smooth, all right, but Chadwell didn't trust him any further than he could heave a longhorn. Maybe he was sincere in what he said; maybe he wasn't. But the man had been with Howell Trainor a long time, and Chadwell knew Trainor well enough to be sure of one thing—the senator wasn't going to let anything stand between him and the governor's chair.

Evan was a smart man, and Chadwell knew that he wouldn't be taken in by Prescott's line. Could be that Evan would learn just as much today as Prescott would.

Besides, Chadwell thought—and the grin returned to his face as he did so—that Kathy Trainor was a real beauty, and it wouldn't do Evan any harm to have a little female companionship. The man was at an age when he ought to be thinking about taking a wife.

"Billy Chadwell, you're a meddling old woman," he told himself aloud. Then he chuckled and went back to work.

Down on the street, Evan and Prescott walked toward Crider's Livery Stable. "Miss Kathy will meet us at the stable," Prescott said. "I've already arranged to rent a couple of horses."

"That's where I keep my horse stabled when I'm in town," Evan said. "I hope you're right about Miss Trainor not being angry with me anymore."

"I'm sure you don't have to worry about that. I think once the two of you get to know each other you'll hit it off quite well. You may even have some mutual friends from the time you were at the university in Austin."

Evan glanced at Prescott and said, "Could be." It seemed that Prescott had done some asking around about him; otherwise he wouldn't have known about Evan's stay in Austin.

They turned a corner, and Evan saw Kathy Trainor standing in front of the livery stable next to a mare that was already saddled. Gunther was with her, as was the maid, Mary Killane.

Prescott smiled as he and Evan walked up to the trio. "I was able to convince Mr. Maddock to join us, Kathy," he said.

"I see," Kathy said coolly. "Hello, Mr. Maddock."

Evan nodded and touched the brim of his hat. "Miss Trainor. Good to see you again."

"Gunther, would you bring out my horse?" Prescott requested, and the big man nodded and went to fetch the animal.

In a low voice that was still audible to Evan, Mary Killane said to Kathy, "Are you sure you want to take this ride, dear? There's been so much trouble already."

"I'm sure there will be no trouble this time," Kathy replied. Her words were directed to Mary, but her eyes were watching Evan. "Not with Mr. Maddock along," she added.

She wasn't as forgiving as Prescott made her out to be, Evan thought. There was an undeniable tension between the two of them—as if she was determined to be polite to him no matter what her true feelings might be. As for him, he didn't know why he was worrying about how some politician's daughter from Austin felt about him. But when he looked at her, so attractive in a fetching riding outfit, complete with little hat perched on her chestnut curls, there was a surge of interest—maybe even desire—that ran through him. It was unbidden, but it was there.

He met her eyes and knew that she had seen him watching her. "Best get my horse saddled up," he said. He went into the stable and met Gunther leading out a horse for Warren Prescott.

It didn't take long for Evan to get his own mount saddled and ready. He swung into the saddle in the shadows of the barn and then rode out to find Prescott and Kathy already mounted up.

"Reckon we can head off to the south and follow the river a ways," Evan said.

"Whatever you like," Prescott said. "We're in your hands, Mr. Maddock."

Gunther and Mary stood in front of the stable and watched the three riders move off down the street. After a moment, Gunther turned to Mary and said, "Now that they're gone, what say you and me take a little walk ourselves?"

Mary looked over at him, lifting an eyebrow in surprise. "And why should I want to do that?"

Gunther looked at her meaningfully. "I can think of several reasons."

For a moment, Mary seemed on the verge of losing her temper and giving him a tongue-lashing. Then her expression abruptly softened. "Well, then," she said, "we'll just have to discuss those reasons, won't we?"

Gunther grinned.

She slipped her arm through his and said, "But I shall expect you to behave like a perfect gentleman, Mr. Wagner. Do you understand?"

"You bet I do," Gunther replied.

They strolled down the street in the direction opposite the one taken by the three riders.

Evan, Prescott, and Kathy Trainor reached the edge of the city and moved out along a trail that followed the broad bed of the river. The river itself was a fairly good size at this time of year, fueled by the spring melt-off of the high snows in the Santa Fe Mountains of New Mexico. Later in the summer, it would shrink to a small trickle in the center of the wide riverbed. The wildflowers were plentiful now, though, and the foliage close to the river was green and healthy.

"This is beautiful country," Kathy said as they rode alongside the river. "At least right here it is. And this is much more pleasant than riding in the hot, dusty stage-coach."

"Yes, a majestic country you have here, Maddock," Prescott said.

"You've got that backward," Evan said, the pleasant tone of his voice taking any sting out of the words. "We don't have the land. The land has us. If we treat it right, it'll let us stay. It can be mighty pretty hereabouts, though." He glanced over at Kathy Trainor. "Yes, sir, mighty pretty."

The look and the words had slipped out almost before he knew what he was saying. He had never been one to sweet-talk the ladies, but something about Kathy Trainor was different from all the women he had met before. He took his eyes off her and looked back at the trail, silently telling himself not to get foolish ideas.

Kathy felt a faint, warm flush of embarrassment. There was no mistaking the meaning behind Evan Maddock's words. In his own way, he was trying to tell her something, and it was a message she wasn't sure she wanted to hear from him. True, he was striking, even handsome in a rough way, and except for the brief fight that Gunther had started, he had exhibited none of the hooligan tactics that had turned her against his family. But she couldn't get out of her mind the fact that his brother had disrupted her father's speech.

Nor was she likely to forget that wild ride in the runaway stagecoach. Not any time soon, at any rate.

She had been shocked when Warren announced his intention of asking Evan to accompany them on this ride. He explained that he wanted to ask Evan about the cur-rent political situation in Reeves County, but Kathy sus-pected that he had more in mind than asking a few simple questions. Her guess would be that Warren was going to try to get Evan's promise that he would deliver his family's votes for Howell Trainor on election day.

Ever the politician, though he held no office. That was Warren Prescott, Kathy thought.

Prescott watched what was going on between Kathy and Evan, and inside he felt a surge of anger. Considering what had happened since the arrival of the Trainor party in Pecos, he hadn't expected the two of them to put aside their differences so easily. Once Kathy had broken the initial tension, she and Evan seemed to be getting along quite well.

That was all right, he sternly told himself. He had plans for Evan Maddock, just as he had plans for Kathy, and he wasn't about to let those plans go astray. For the moment, he would just have to be patient and let Evan continue trying to charm Kathy.

In the end, there would be only one winner. Warren Prescott.

Right now he had to keep up appearances, so he began asking Evan the questions that had served as his ruse to draw the young lawyer out here. Evan proved to be a keen observer of what was going on politically in the county, though he protested that he wasn't really interested in such matters and was content with the law practice. Kathy joined in the discussion as well, and Prescott and Evan were both impressed with her knowledge of the political process. She was her father's daughter, right enough, with a quick intelligence of her own.

After a few miles, the trail branched, one leg of it turning away from the river and heading more directly southward. Kathy pointed at the branch leading away through the chaparral and asked, "Where does that lead?"

"Another few miles down the trail is the ranch my brothers and I own," Evan said. "The other side of that is my Uncle Axel's spread."

"The one whose men were being chased by the Lindsays that day they stampeded the stagecoach?" Kathy asked with a small frown.

"I'm afraid so," Evan answered after a second's pause.

He hadn't wanted to bring up any bad memories; he was enjoying Kathy's company too much.

A long moment passed, and then Kathy said, "I've never been on a real ranch before. Would you mind showing me around yours?"

Evan stopped himself from heaving a sigh of relief in reaction to her continued friendliness. "Sure," he said. "Be glad to."

The three of them turned down the trail to the Maddock ranch. Evan was going to enjoy showing her around the ranch; it was a good spread, something to be proud of even though he had little to do with its day-to-day operation.

They hadn't ridden more than half a mile when Evan suddenly saw something that made him frown and narrow his eyes in concentration. A grim feeling took hold of him as he tried to make out a shape lying just to the side of the road in the brush, about fifty yards ahead of them.

It looked almighty like a man's body.

Evan reined in and said, "Hold up a minute."

Kathy and Prescott brought their horses to a stop, and Prescott asked, "Is something wrong?"

"Why don't the two of you stay here a minute?" Evan said, his tone hard. "There's something I want to check out."

"All right, but—" Before Prescott could finish, Evan was spurring away, prodding his horse into a gallop.

Evan covered ground quickly, reining in hard as he came even with the sprawled body. There was no doubt about it now. The man was lying facedown and not moving.

Evan swung down from the saddle, glancing up at the sky as he did so. For the first time he noticed the grotesque shapes circling high in the bright sky. He cursed himself; he'd been spending too much time in town—either that or he was getting blind not to have seen the vultures.

For a moment as he rode down the trail, the ice-cold fear that this was Johnny's body gripped him. His brother rode this trail often, and Johnny had been in town last night. But now he saw that the clothes weren't Johnny's.

As Evan knelt by the body, he saw the irregular rise and fall of the man's back. He was still alive.

Evan reached out, grasped the man's shoulder, and rolled him over as gently as possible. The shock of recognition hit him as he saw Matt Lindsay's face.

Matt's breathing was ragged and harsh, and there was a large crimson stain high on the left side of his body. He had been shot, probably by a handgun.

Evan stared down at Matt's pale, sweat-beaded face for a long moment. There had never been any trouble between him and Matt, other than the fact of their last names and that damned feud.

He knew that he couldn't leave him out here to die. He would have to take Matt back into Pecos to the doctor.

Evan stood up and waved for Kathy and Trainor to come closer. As he waited for them, another thought abruptly occurred to him. Matt and Johnny had nearly drawn on each other the night before, according to Billy Chadwell. Was it possible that Johnny had done this?

Was Johnny's body lying somewhere close by?

As the realization of that possibility came to Evan, he felt his heart begin to pound against his ribs. He cast his eyes up and down the trail, but he saw nothing else. He turned and pushed his way into the brush as Prescott and Kathy rode up.

Prescott quickly dismounted, saying, "You stay back, Kathy." Both of them had seen the wounded man by this time. Prescott called to Evan, "What's going on, Maddock?"

"That man's been shot," Evan answered over his shoulder. "We'll have to get him back to town."

"What are you looking for?" Kathy asked from the back of her horse. She had paled a bit at the sight of the blood on Matt Lindsay's shirt, but she was holding herself together well.

Evan didn't answer her, but a moment later they both heard the strangled cry. "Nooo!" he wailed, and it was the sound of a man in agony.

"My God!" Prescott exclaimed. He pushed into the chaparral, following the path made by Evan. Though she was almost as afraid as when the stagecoach had run away, Kathy dropped from her saddle and went after him.

They found Evan Maddock on his knees, next to the body of his brother.

Johnny Maddock was lying facedown in the sand, unmoving. He would never move again.

Evan's hat had fallen from his head, and as he stared down at Johnny's body his face was locked in a grimace of grief and pain. His mind was numb. It was obvious what had happened. Johnny's body was only a few yards from where Matt Lindsay had fallen. The two young men had continued their fight from where it left off in the Flores Cantina.

And now Johnny was dead, while Matt Lindsay still lived.

Evan came to his feet, pushed roughly past Prescott and Kathy, and ran to his horse. They looked after him in confusion and saw him jerk the Winchester from the boot on his saddle.

He levered a shell into the chamber, his fingers trembling from the rage inside him. He raised the rifle and lined the sights on Matt Lindsay.

His eyes blurred and his hands shook, so the aim was slow in coming. Then he thought again about what he was doing. He lowered the rifle. Matt Lindsay may have murdered Johnny, but still he was due a trial by jury to prove his guilt.

Evan shook his head. In the heat of his anger, even he had been ready to take the law into his own hands before his reason had reasserted itself.

Kathy moved past Prescott. She saw the pain etched on Evan's face, and though they had had their differences in the past, today had showed her a different side of him. She was starting to like him. And now she was drawn to comfort him.

She put her hand on his arm. "I'm so sorry, Evan," she said softly. "I'm so sorry."

Evan looked down at her, but his eyes seemed to be seeing something else . . . *A handsome young man, laugh-*

ing, too sure of himself for his own good but still full of life . . .

"He said you were one of the prettiest women he'd ever seen," Evan told her, almost in a whisper.

The sound of hoofbeats, a lot of them, came to their ears. A large group of riders was pounding down the trail.

Evan looked up dully at the newcomers. There were a dozen cowhands on horseback, and he recognized them as the crew from his ranch. They were led by two riders, one of them a blond-haired teenage boy, the other a burly, black-bearded bear of a man.

"Evan!" the boy cried out as he reined up and leaped from the saddle. "Evan, have you seen Johnny?"

The bearded man, Nacho Newcomb, stayed on his horse and said, "Johnny's horse came back to the ranch this morning without him. We've been out looking for him." Nacho spat in the dirt, looked at Matt Lindsay, and went on, "Lindsay got himself shot, did he?"

Evan jerked his head toward the brush. "Johnny's in there," he said hoarsely.

The blond-headed boy started toward the chaparral, but Evan caught him by the arm.

"You don't want to go in there, Ted," he said.

Ted Maddock looked up into the face of his oldest brother and read the awful truth there. He blinked back tears and forced himself to put it into words. "He's dead, isn't he?"

Evan nodded.

Ted tried to hold it back, but a sob wracked him. Evan drew the boy against him and folded his arms around him, the two brothers trying to take comfort from each other in this moment of grief.

In a soft voice filled with great feeling, Nacho said, "Damn!" He climbed down from the saddle as the other hands cursed in muffled tones. Pushing his way into the brush with his broad, powerful body, Nacho came to Johnny's lifeless form and knelt beside it. There was no mistake. Johnny was dead, and Nacho felt like a part of himself had died along with the boy.

Nacho Newcomb had worked on the Maddock ranch

for nearly thirty years, since he was just a boy himself. He had seen Maddock sons born, and he had seen Maddock sons die. He had risen to the position of foreman, but in actuality he was a member of the family after all these years.

He stood up and strode out of the chaparral, and the look on his face was fierce. He stopped next to Evan. "Lindsay do that?" he asked.

"Looks like it," Evan replied as he held onto Ted.

Moving with a speed startling in one so large, the English-Mexican vaquero whipped out the bowie knife on his hip and knelt next to Matt Lindsay. His fingers tangled in Matt's hair, and he jerked the head back, exposing the throat for a fatal slash of the big knife.

"Nacho, no!" Evan yelled. He knew all too well how close he had come to killing Matt Lindsay only moments before, but now his reason had regained control.

Nacho stopped the blade just above Matt's throat. A moan of pain slipped from Matt's lips, though he didn't regain consciousness.

"The law will handle it," Evan heard himself saying. "But we'll need evidence. Nacho, get Lindsay's gun . . . and I suppose we'll need Johnny's, too."

Nacho looked over his shoulder at Evan. Then with a snarl of rage he released Matt Lindsay's head. He stood up and slipped the bowie back in its sheath and then took the gun from the unconscious man's hand.

"I remember a time when the only law was justice," he growled.

"There will be justice," Evan promised.

Warren Prescott spoke up for the first time since the arrival of the group from the ranch. "I'm sorry, Maddock. I'm terribly sorry about your brother. But we'd better get this man into town before he bleeds to death."

"You're right." Evan nodded. "Nacho, have some of the boys load Matt on a horse. And take it easy with him!" he added sharply.

"Sí," Nacho muttered. He motioned for some of the hands to help him.

Evan put his hands on Ted's shoulders and looked

down into his face. Ted was trying to stop crying, and with a loud sniff he brought himself under control.

"Ted, this is Miss Trainor and Mr. Prescott," Evan told him. "Why don't you mount up and ride along with them? Nacho and the boys and I will be along in a few minutes."

"You . . . you'll bring Johnny?" Ted asked.

"We'll bring Johnny," Evan said bleakly. The pain was still tearing at him inside, but he had to be strong for Ted's sake. He was all the boy had left now.

Kathy stepped forward and put her hand on Ted's shoulder. "My name is Kathy, Ted," she told him in a soft voice. "You come along with me." She gently led him away.

A few minutes later, the whole group started back up the trail to Pecos, two of the ranch hands doubling up with their friends so that Johnny and Matt could be loaded on horseback. It was a somber procession.

And all of them knew that after the morning, things would never be the same in Pecos again.

Chapter Seven

Gunther Wagner was whistling an off-key tune as he polished the brass fittings of the special stagecoach with a soft cloth. His walk with Mary Killane had put him in a good mood, causing his usual glower to be replaced by a little grin.

Mary was different from those women to whom Gunther was accustomed. He had always preferred a more . . . *earthy* type for his female companionship. But Mary was cute as a button and smart, and she was one to speak her mind. Gunther had been attracted to her ever since she had come to work for the senator a few months ago, and he had decided before this journey began that he was going to break through the shell she had built around her.

He had to go slow, though, and that was difficult for him. The walk with her today and the way she had thawed out a bit as they talked were the first encouraging signs. He was starting to believe that maybe he could charm her, given time.

And besides, he thought with a grin, sometimes the ones who were frosty on the surface like that were hot with passion once they were thawed out.

It was hot enough in this barn, that was for sure. Gunther paused to wipe his forearm over his sweaty forehead, and then he put down the polishing cloth and peeled his shirt up and over his head. Bare to the waist, he went back to work.

"Mr. Wagner!" a shocked voice exclaimed behind him.

He turned around quickly and saw Mary emerging

from the shadows. "Oh. I, uh, didn't hear you come in, Miss Killane," he said. "Sorry about the way I look."

"Your appearance is hardly decorous," she began sternly and then paused. "But I suppose when a man is working in a hot barn, there are more important things than decorum."

"Uh . . . right." Gunther wasn't sure whether to be embarrassed or not. He was acutely aware of the fact that he was alone in the barn with this woman and that he was half naked. She didn't seem to mind, though, once she had gotten over her initial surprise; in fact, she was looking at him now with something very much like admiration.

"You have the most extraordinary musculature, Mr. Wagner," Mary said, coming closer to him.

"Well, I've always worked hard," he said, uncertain whether or not he should back up.

"In fact, you remind me somewhat of pictures I've seen of the statues in ancient Greece." She was close to him now, only about a foot away.

"Lord, that was a quick thaw," Gunther muttered under his breath.

"What did you say, Mr. Wagner?"

"I, uh, said I wouldn't know anything about ancient Greece, ma'am."

"Then perhaps I could increase your knowledge of fine culture, Mr. Wagner. And why don't you call me Mary?"

Suddenly there was shouting in the street outside, and Gunther took advantage of the commotion. "Sure, Mary," he said and then ducked away from her. "I'd better see what's going on."

She followed him to the door of the livery stable, and they both saw the group of riders coming at a walk down the main street of Pecos. They saw Kathy and Prescott, and they saw the two bodies draped motionless over saddles. Mary's hand went to her mouth. "Oh, dear God," she whispered. "What's happened?"

Gunther pulled his shirt on and stalked out into the street, his face grim, and fell into step beside Prescott's horse. "Are you and Miss Kathy all right, sir?" he asked.

"We're fine, Gunther," Prescott replied. "But there's been some trouble, bad trouble."

"Anything I can do to help?"

"No, I don't think so. I'm not sure any of us can help with this trouble."

Gunther stopped and watched as the riders moved on down the street. Townspeople ran along the sidewalk, drawn by the sight of the bodies, and shouted questions to each other and to the Maddock ranch hands.

Evan was leading the horse with Johnny's body draped over it. He reined in when he reached the little frame building that housed the city's only undertaker. Ted and Nacho stopped as well.

"We'll take care of this," Evan said to the hands in a level voice. "The rest of you boys take Matt on down to the doc's."

"All right, Evan," one of the hands said. "We'll sure do it."

The hands jogged their horses into motion again as Evan, Ted, and Nacho dismounted. Gently, carefully, Evan and Nacho took Johnny down from the horse that bore him and carried the boy into the undertaker's parlor.

Kathy and Prescott were left sitting their horses in front of the undertaker's. Prescott said, "I don't think there's anything else we can do to help here, Kathy. Why don't we go on back to the hotel?"

"All right," she nodded. She had cried a bit herself on seeing Ted Maddock's reaction to his brother's death, and her eyes were slightly red. "This feud is a horrible thing, Warren."

"Yes, it is," he agreed. "Perhaps the end result of this killing will be to put a stop to it, though."

"What makes you think that?"

"Nothing." He reined his horse around. "Just speculating."

He walked the horse on toward the hotel, Kathy at his side. He had almost spoken too much, revealed too much of his plan. In the future, he would have to be more careful. There was nothing like a beautiful woman to loosen a man's tongue.

Howell Trainor, in shirt-sleeves and vest, was in the sitting room of the hotel suite going over the itinerary for the rest of the campaign trip when Kathy and Prescott entered the room. He looked up, saw the grim set of their faces, and knew immediately that something was wrong.

"What is it?" he said as he stood up.

"Oh, Daddy, it was awful," Kathy said, sniffling again now. "Johnny Maddock is dead."

"Maddock?" Trainor frowned. "The one who interrupted my speech last night?"

"I'm afraid so, sir," Prescott replied. He took off his hat. "It appears that young Maddock and one of the Lindsays shot each other on the trail outside of town."

"My God! Are they both dead?"

Prescott shook his head. "The Lindsay boy is still alive. He's at the doctor's office now; I don't know how badly he's hurt. Evan Maddock was the one who found them, while the three of us were out riding."

Trainor shot a glance at Kathy. "You saw?"

She nodded, wiped away a tear, and faced her father. "I saw it."

Trainor put his arms around his daughter and drew her to him. "I'm sorry, darling. I knew we should have left this place before you were exposed to another dreadful scene."

Kathy shook her head and declared, "I'm all right now. It was just hard seeing how it affected Evan and his little brother. Ted and some of the ranch hands came up right after we found the bodies. I felt so sorry for him and for Evan."

"No good ever comes of such violence," Trainor said. "People who resort to it are bound to come to bad ends." He sighed. "I was certainly angry at the boy last night, but I'm sorry to hear that he's dead."

Kathy slipped out of her father's arms and walked slowly to the window overlooking the street. She looked down toward the undertaker's parlor and saw Evan, Ted, and Nacho emerge from the little building. The three of them began walking up the street toward the hotel. Nacho had his hand on the boy's shoulder; Evan walked alone, his face set in tight lines.

Kathy saw them push through the crowd that was gathered on the sidewalk outside the doctor's office. When the townspeople saw who was trying to get through, they stepped back and made way. Evan and Nacho went inside, but Ted stayed outside with one of the ranch hands after Evan spoke briefly to the man.

"Warren?" Kathy said.

"Yes, Kathy?"

"Evan Maddock just went into the doctor's office. I . . . I wish you'd go down there and make sure that nothing else happens."

Trainor said, "You're afraid he'll try to settle things with Lindsay?"

"I'd say that's a legitimate fear," Prescott answered. "Of course I'll go down there, Kathy."

"Darling, will you be all right here by yourself?" Trainor asked Kathy. She nodded, and he went on, "I think I should go with Warren. Perhaps we should fetch the sheriff. This situation might get ugly." Trainor cast a glance at the crowd in front of the doctor's office.

"Good idea, sir," Prescott agreed. He put his hat back on while Trainor slipped into his coat and picked up his own hat.

The two men hurried downstairs and started across the street. Before they reached the doctor's office, their path intersected with that of Sheriff Issac Ring, who had also heard the commotion and had come to see what was going on.

"Howdy, Senator," Ring said, nodding. He indicated the mob with a jerk of his head. "You got any notion what caused this ruckus?"

Prescott answered instead of Trainor. "Johnny Maddock has been killed, Sheriff. He and Matt Lindsay shot it out on the trail to the Maddock ranch."

Ring let out a whistle. "Holeee . . . I reckon Matt must still be alive and in the doc's office, judging by that mess of people. Who found 'em?"

"Evan Maddock," Prescott said. "He and I were out

riding with Senator Trainor's daughter when we found them. Evan's in the doctor's office now."

"Damn!" Ring exclaimed. "I'd best get in there, too." He strode toward the crowd on the sidewalk, raising his voice and calling, "Make way there! Let me through, dammit!"

The sheriff pushed his way past the townspeople clogging the doorway and stalked into the doctor's office. Trainor and Prescott took advantage of the cleared path and followed closely on Ring's heels.

Matt Lindsay was stretched out on the doctor's examining table, his shirt off and his left shoulder a bloody mess. The doctor was bent over him, probing at the wound. Evan and Nacho were standing by and waiting, a few feet away from the table. Evan's face was haggard and drawn, but he seemed to be under control, as was Nacho Newcomb.

"Got to get that bullet out," the doctor grunted without looking up. "That's the most important thing right now."

Sheriff Ring stepped over to Evan and said in a low voice, "Hate to bother you right now, son, but you reckon you could tell me what happened?"

Before Evan could answer, the doctor said sharply, "Let it wait a minute, Ike. I've got to concentrate on what I'm doing here."

"Sorry, Doc."

A few minutes later, the doctor straightened up and held out his bloodied hand. A misshapen slug lay in the palm. "There it is," he said. "Not too much damage, I'd say. Matt's shoulder will always be stiff, but he'll live, all right."

"Good," Evan snapped. "Sheriff, you'll need that bullet as evidence, along with the one that killed my brother. I want this done right. I want Lindsay to stand trial for murder and then *hang*."

Sheriff Ike Ring spoke up, "Evan, how'd you find the two of 'em?"

"They were both in the brush beside the trail heading

out to my ranch," Evan said. "Matt was closest to the road. He was alive. Johnny was dead."

Ring shook his head. "I'm sorry, Evan, but you know that don't make it murder. Johnny could have started the fight, and still it could've ended that way. You say he was deeper in the brush; could he have been layin' in wait for Matt?"

For a moment, Evan just looked at the sheriff and again felt as if he were going to explode. But then he caught sight of Nacho Newcomb and remembered the gun the foreman had taken from Lindsay's hand. "Nacho, let's see the evidence," he said.

Nacho Newcomb stepped forward and took a Colt revolver from where it was tucked under his belt. He held the gun out to Evan, who took it and said to the sheriff, "This is Matt's gun. It was lying in his hand. Thought you might want to see it. Nacho has Johnny's gun, too."

Ring checked the cylinder of Matt Lindsay's Colt. "Two shots fired," he grunted.

Nacho took another gun from his belt and held it out to the sheriff. "This one's Johnny's. You can see for yourself, there's just been one shot fired."

"True enough," Ring admitted after looking the weapon over.

Trainor spoke up then, unable to keep quiet any longer. "I don't understand," he said. "Why does it matter how many shots were fired?"

Ring glanced at the politician and then stowed both guns away under his belt. "One bullet in each man, three shots fired. One shot had to've missed." He didn't feel obliged to explain any further. He hadn't known that Trainor and Prescott were going to follow him in here; if he had, he might have stopped them. But they were here now, and Trainor swung too much weight for Ike Ring to boot him out.

"It's plain enough what happened!" Evan said angrily. "And I intend to prove it in court."

At that moment Billy Chadwell pushed into the room, glaring at Evan. Evan took a deep breath and tightened the rein on his anger. Billy's unvoiced criticism was valid, of course. Matt Lindsay was innocent until proven guilty in a court of law. Evan had always upheld that premise, and he knew he had to stick to it now, though another part of him wanted to strangle Matt Lindsay on the spot. But if his belief in the legal system were at all justified, he would have to abide by it no matter who was involved.

Ring held up his hands. "Let's just hold on here, folks. I've heard how Johnny and Matt were found, and I know they almost got into a shooting scrape last night, but I can't go charging anybody with anything until I've talked to Matt and heard his side of it."

As if on cue, Matt let out a moan and began to toss his head from side to side. With a firm grip on his shoulders, the doctor held him still.

"Can we talk to him?" the sheriff quickly asked, stepping forward.

The doctor glanced up in anger. "He's hurt and he needs rest. I should give him an injection to make him sleep."

"Sorry, but I need answers, Doc."

The doctor sighed. "All right." He held up a warning finger. "But only for a few minutes. Nacho, you hold him still so that he doesn't do himself any more damage."

Nacho moved around to the head of the examining table and put his hamlike hands on Matt's shoulders. The vaquero's enormous strength was more than adequate to keep the wounded man from moving around.

Ring leaned over Matt and said in a loud voice, "Can you hear me, Lindsay? Lindsay!"

Matt's eyelids fluttered open, and he tried to lick his lips. He croaked, "Wh-whuh yuh want?"

"This is Sheriff Ike Ring, boy. I want to know why you killed Johnny Maddock."

"M-Maddock. . . ? Don' unnerstand. . . *Uh!*"

Matt winced, a spasm of pain obviously passing through him, and Nacho bore down harder on his shoulders to keep him still.

The doctor moved around Nacho's bulk and, before anyone could stop him, jabbed a needle into Matt's arm.

"Dammit, I'm talkin' to this man!" the sheriff complained. "I don't need you knockin' him out, Doc!"

"I said you could question him for a few minutes," the doctor replied coolly. "He'll still be awake for a few minutes before the medicine puts him under, and he'll be more coherent than if I hadn't given him the injection. I suggest you not waste any more time, Sheriff."

Ring glowered at the doctor and rubbed a hand along his stubbly jaw. Then he leaned close to Matt Lindsay again.

The pain having eased some already, Matt looked around him with eyes that were more aware of what he was seeing. "Wh-what is this?" he asked. "What's happened?"

"You've been shot in the shoulder, boy," Ring told him. "Do you remember how it happened?"

Matt shook his head gingerly. "Don't remember anything. You said something . . . something about Johnny Maddock?"

Evan stepped forward. "You don't remember killing him, huh?" he blazed, hands involuntarily clenching into fists. Chadwell put a hand on his arm to restrain him.

"Don't know . . . what you're talkin' about."

"Do you remember trying to get Johnny to draw on you in the Flores Cantina last night?" the sheriff asked.

"S-sure. 'Member that all right."

"And after that? What happened then?"

Matt's eyes were drooping now as the drug took hold. "Went to . . . to the Double Eagle, had some more to drink. Good time, lots of booze . . . Thass all I 'member . . ." His voice trailed off.

"You've got to remember more than that!" Evan burst out. Chadwell put his hand on Evan's arm, as though to quiet him.

Ike Ring shook his head. "No use yelling at him, Maddock. He's out; he can't hear you. Chadwell, you and your partner can leave now. Newcomb, you too."

Evan took a deep breath. "All right, Sheriff. We'll leave. But I'll want to talk to you outside."

"Figured you would," Ring replied with a sigh.

Flanked by Chadwell and Nacho, Evan walked out of the doctor's office, pushed his way through the eagerly watching crowd, and put both hands on the hitching rack. He leaned his weight on the rough-hewn pole and stared down unseeingly at the dusty street.

Nearby was the group of hands from the ranch. Ted was with them, his eyes dry now. The young boy's features were drawn. He came over to Evan, stood beside him, and asked, "What are you going to do about this, Evan?"

Before Evan could answer, Chadwell said, "There's nothing more any of us can do right now, Ted. Why don't you and Evan go back out to the ranch and try to get some rest?"

Evan shook his head. "I'm not tired, Billy." He laughed harshly. "Hell, it's only the middle of the day. Besides, I told Ike Ring I wanted to talk to him."

Chadwell sighed. "All right. If there's anything I can do to help, Evan, you know all you have to do is ask. Shoot, you don't even have to do that much."

Evan looked over at his partner and read the concern evident on Chadwell's face. "Thanks, Billy," he said, and meant it. "We'll be all right."

Chadwell nodded. "I know."

Sheriff Ring came out onto the porch and held up his hands under a barrage of questions from the townspeople. "Clear out o' here!" he barked. "Go on back to your homes and businesses and let the law do its work, all right?"

Slowly, the crowd dispersed. Ring hooked his thumbs in his belt and came over to the hitching rack, where Evan, Ted, Chadwell, and Nacho waited.

"Sheriff, I want the trial to be held right away," Evan demanded. "If we delay—"

Ring interrupted him, saying, "Reckon we'd better let Mr. Hadley decide the next move." He nodded toward a man who was hurrying down the street in their direction, wearing a suit and a pair of thick-lensed glasses. "After all, he is the district attorney."

Stephen Hadley came up to the little group and said,

"What is this, Sheriff? I was told that a murder had been committed."

"You heard right," Evan said before Ring could reply.

"Now just hold on a minute," the sheriff drawled. "I've got the story now, Maddock, so I'll fill Mr. Hadley in on what's happened."

Quickly, Ring laid out the facts. The district attorney listened with a growing frown on his face. When the sheriff reached the end of the story, Hadley pulled a handkerchief from his pocket and mopped his forehead. "This is bad," he said. "This is very bad."

"Yes, it is. And the sooner you charge Matt Lindsay and he stands trial for murder, the better," Evan asserted.

Hadley pushed his glasses up on his nose. "I'm not sure. Matt might claim it was self-defense—"

"I hope to prove that he fired first," Evan insisted. "That's not self-defense."

"You don't know it happened that way," Ring pointed out. "Just because he fired one more shot than Johnny don't mean he fired first. Johnny could have ambushed him."

Scorn was heavy in Evan's voice as he said, "Johnny wouldn't ambush anybody, and you know it, Sheriff."

"He never did strike me as the type; that's true enough."

"Matt must have followed him out of town," Evan went on. "Johnny tried to get into the brush and stay out of a fight. He was drunk, too, but smart enough to know he didn't have any business pulling a gun in that condition. Matt forced the fight, though—just like he tried to do earlier in the saloon—and missed with his first shot. That's the way it had to be."

"That theory makes sense, Evan," Hadley said, "but I don't know how you'd prove it. I'm afraid unless we can find another witness, the only one who knows for sure what happened out there is Matt Lindsay."

"And he claims he don't remember," Ring put in.

"But that doesn't mean he shouldn't stand trial," Evan replied. He was vaguely aware that Trainor and Prescott had come out of the doctor's office and were listening to what was being said.

"I just don't know," Hadley said worriedly. "If I charge Matt with murder, and it can't be proven, old Jubal wouldn't take kindly to my arresting his boy on a charge that didn't hold up."

Nacho Newcomb spoke up. "If you're afraid of Jubal Lindsay, you just think about how Axel is going to act when he finds out that a Lindsay killed Johnny."

Hadley shot an angry glance at the big foreman. "I'm not afraid of Jubal Lindsay, Mr. Newcomb," he said firmly. "Neither am I afraid of Axel Maddock. I am afraid of the repercussions this incident could have on the city, though."

"This isn't just an *incident*, Mr. Hadley." Evan's voice was cold. "Our brother is dead, and Ted and I want to see his killer tried and convicted. I realize that as Johnny's brother I can't prosecute this case myself, but that doesn't change the fact that it is the responsibility of the court to sort through the facts and decide the issue. The people of this county *expect* justice."

A new voice abruptly injected itself into the discussion. "That is why we have a legal system, after all. Excuse me, gentlemen," Warren Prescott said, "I know I'm a stranger in these parts, but it appears to me that you have a classic dilemma here."

"These men don't need a lecture on the legal system," Trainor snapped to his aide. "But I *do* agree. A trial is always the best means of arriving at the truth."

"I just don't know," Hadley said, a thoughtful look on his face. "If we have a trial here, it's likely to stir up the feud even worse and cause more bloodshed. I'd feel a whole lot better if the defense would request a change of venue. If the trial were held in another city—hell, another *county*—then local feelings wouldn't be ignited quite so much."

Evan shook his head. "No. I strongly disagree, Hadley. The people of this city need to see once and for all that the legal system does work, and that the courts are the place for arguments to be settled. They want to see justice done, but too many of them don't believe it will be done in the courts. This is our chance to change their minds. I say the *only* way to avoid more bloodshed is to hold the trial right here in Pecos."

"You've got something there, Evan," Billy Chadwell said. "Maybe you couldn't prove the case right now, Hadley, but you could go ahead and charge Matt and hold him. That would give you time to investigate and maybe keep the Maddocks and the Lindsays from burning the city."

"Exactly!" Prescott interjected. He hadn't counted on Evan Maddock himself arguing for a trial, not with his brother killed, but he wasn't going to turn down the assistance, inadvertant as it might be.

Hadley rubbed his jaw and pondered the situation. "I just don't know," he said musingly.

"I can understand your reluctance," Prescott said. "You're a public official. You can't take sides in something like this feud."

"The feud doesn't matter," Evan said hotly. "You've got a duty to prosecute killers, Hadley."

"It's a shame you can't get someone from outside the county to handle the case," Prescott said. "If you could, that would eliminate any question of prejudice."

"Yes," Trainor agreed quickly. "A special prosecutor might be just the answer to your problem."

"You think so?" Hadley's voice was eager. He wanted desperately to find some way out of this predicament, so that he could go back to his normal, placid job. He was just a country lawyer at heart, and he felt out of his element in any situation this complicated and charged with danger.

"I'm sure of it," Trainor assured him. His mind was working along familiar lines now. The years spent campaigning for various offices had taught him always to be on the lookout for anything that would get his name before the public in a good light. If he could win a spectacular murder case that would draw the attention of the press . . .

"I could call in a few favors in Austin and get the state attorney general to appoint me as a special prosecutor,"

Trainor said, pushing ahead now that the idea had occurred to him.

"That way no one could question the fairness of the
trial. After all, you have no ties with either of the families
involved," Hadley said, nodding. "What do you think,
Ike?"

"I just want to get to the bottom of this mess," Ring
answered. "Don't really care how we go about it, long as
we can keep the peace."

"What do you say, Maddock?" Prescott asked Evan.

Evan looked from face to face in the group and knew
that their minds were made up. As for himself, he wasn't
so certain. He felt as if he were caught in a flash flood of
tragedy that was sweeping all of them along to some
unknowable conclusion. The only one who might come
out ahead was Howell Trainor, who knew how to turn any
situation to his advantage, no matter how bad it was or
how much it hurt other people. Evan thought maybe he
was just being cynical—but perhaps he was being realistic.
Turning back to the district attorney, he asked, "Matt'll be
charged with murder?"

"For now, yes," Hadley told him. "Later on, if the
evidence uncovered warrants it, we might reduce the
charge to manslaughter."

"All right. I just want to see him stand trial soon."

"We'll all do our best, Mr. Maddock," Trainor told
him. "I give you my word on that."

Young Ted Maddock watched the adults around him,
trying to take in the points they were discussing, and
suddenly he said, "That's all you're going to do?" His
voice was choked with pain and anger.

"That's all we can do right now, Ted," Chadwell told
him.

"It's settled, then," Trainor said. "Mr. Hadley, if you
and Sheriff Ring agree, I'd like to get started." He had
already taken charge, and none of the others were going to
object, at least not yet.

Trainor, Hadley, and Ring moved off down the street,
discussing the case among themselves. Warren Prescott

hung back for just a moment and permitted himself a satisfied smile that none of the others could see.

Trainor was as easy to manipulate as ever. So far, the plan was working out just fine.

As Prescott followed after the others, Evan Maddock turned to his brother. "Come on, Ted," he said. "Let's ride on out to the ranch." He didn't feel like staying in town, not today, not after what had happened.

Evan, Ted, and Nacho rejoined the group of Maddock hands and mounted their horses. Evan turned to Chadwell and said, "I'll talk to you later, Billy."

Chadwell nodded and lifted a hand in farewell as the group rode slowly out of town.

As Evan and the others rode past the hotel, Kathy Trainor watched them from the window of her suite. She saw that Evan's face was still full of the pain of Johnny's death. And for some reason, Kathy felt Evan's pain as if it were her own.

Chapter Eight

"**S**tay with him, damn you!" Axel Maddock shouted to the cowboy who was trying to stick to the saddle of a fishtailing horse in the big main corral. The horse was a wild mustang that his men had captured the week before, and it was proving to be almighty hard to break.

Several of the other hands were gathered around the corral, some of them perched on the top rail, as the horse bucked and leaped around the enclosure. They cheered and hooted at the rider and let out a great whoop of derision as the horse switched ends in midair and unseated him. The cowboy landed with a thump in the dust.

Axel shook his head in admiration for the animal. When he had come to this part of the country, huge herds of the wild mustangs had roamed the plains. Now they were almost all gone, and it was rare that one like this was captured.

The sound of pounding hoofbeats took Axel's attention off the corral and the horse inside it. He turned to see one of his hands galloping toward him on a lathered, winded animal. The man was yelling something—something about Johnny. . . .

Dead.

The word lashed out at Axel like a slap across the face.

Reining in hard, the rider brought his horse to a skidding stop and then leaped down from the saddle. "Mr. Maddock!" he called as he ran toward Axel. "Johnny's dead, boss! I just heard it in town!"

Axel reached out and caught at the man's arm with a

bony hand. "Johnny Maddock, you mean?" he demanded. "What the hell are you talkin' about, boy?"

"Yes, sir, Johnny Maddock." The man paused to draw a deep breath; he had obviously ridden hard all the way from Pecos. "He's been shot."

Despite the sun beating down fiercely, Axel felt cold. "Who shot him?"

"The way I heard it, Matt Lindsay's the one who done it. They got him in town, at the doc's office. He's shot, too."

Axel's face hardened until it looked like weathered and creased granite. "Lindsay," he said softly. "I might'a knowed it."

He had never been close to Johnny Maddock, but from what he had seen of the boy, Johnny had had some of the grit that was sadly lacking in his brother Evan. And now he was dead, struck down by a stinking Lindsay.

Axel swung toward the corral. "Saddle up!" he barked at the hands gathered there. When they were slow to move and stared at him in puzzlement, anger flared within him. "Saddle up, goddamn it!" he roared. "And get your guns, all of you. We've got us a score to settle."

With that, he strode away from the corral, back toward the big house. He was going to fetch the Winchester that hung in his study. That gun had disposed of many varmints over the years, and now it was going to help him get rid of one more.

He was going to bring justice to Matt Lindsay. Maddock justice—hangrope justice!

Looking at the ranch house on the Lindsay spread north of Pecos, it was easy to tell that there had been no woman's touch here for many years. From the peeling paint on the outside to the cluttered mess inside, this was the house of a man who cared nothing for appearances.

Jubal Lindsay strode out onto the sagging planks of the front porch and glared at the rider who had galloped up calling his name.

"What the hell's all the yellin' about?" Jubal asked around the wad of tobacco in his cheek.

The rider took his hat off and wiped his sleeve across his sweating face. "I come from town as quick as I could, Mr. Lindsay," he said. "Matt's been hurt."

Jubal frowned. "Hurt? Hurt how bad?"

The rider shook his head. "Don't know for sure, boss. He was shot, I know that much. They took him in the doctor's office."

"Shot?" Jubal's eyes widened in outrage. "Who shot my boy?"

"Johnny Maddock."

A red mist seemed to settle over everything as fury burst inside Jubal. "Maddock!" he howled, and the outcry brought men running from the bunkhouse.

"That's not the worse of it, Mr. Lindsay," the rider said hesitantly.

"Spit it out, man!"

"Johnny Maddock's dead, and I heard that Evan Maddock said they should hang Matt for murderin' him."

Jubal's normally swarthy face became an even deeper shade of brick red as his veins threatened to pop. "Evan Maddock said that, did he?" Automatically, Jubal's hand went to the smooth butt of the old Navy Colt holstered at his hip. "Saddle up!" he snapped at the men gathered in front of the ranch house, unknowingly echoing the command given by Axel Maddock. "We're ridin' for town! Anybody who thinks he's goin' to lynch my boy is dead wrong!"

Jubal's mind was a jumble of emotions as he threw a saddle on his own horse, but rage at the Maddocks was the overriding reaction to this news.

Matt might not amount to a whole hell of a lot, but he was a Lindsay, by God! And no Maddock was going to string up a Lindsay.

If Matt was dead by the time they reached Pecos, Jubal vowed to himself, this whole county was going to be full of powder smoke and blood.

Billy Chadwell walked into the doctor's office and frowned as he looked around for Matt Lindsay. The doctor was at his desk, but there was no sign of the injured man.

"Where's Matt, Doc?" Chadwell asked. "You put him to bed in your back room or something?"

The doctor looked up with an angry expression and then sighed. He took off his glasses and rubbed his eyes. "Matt's over at the jail," he said.

"At the jail?" Chadwell exclaimed. "He didn't look like he was in any shape to be moved."

"That's what I told Ike Ring. But he insisted. Said if Matt was going to be charged with murder, then he wanted him someplace where a lynch mob couldn't get to him. He claimed he could defend the jail a lot easier than he could this office."

"Well, that makes sense, I suppose."

"And Matt should be all right over there. He lost some blood and got some muscles torn up by the bullet, but he should heal just fine. I'll look in on him several times a day."

"Thanks, Doc. I guess I'll go on over to the jail. I want to talk to Matt some more."

The doctor pulled a watch from his pocket and glanced at it. "He won't be waking up for a little while yet. Slept right through it when Ring had his deputies carry him out on a stretcher." He snorted. "Probably a good thing he is out of here. I don't want a bunch of feud-crazy Maddocks and Lindsays shooting up my office."

"I just hope they don't shoot up the whole city." Chadwell sighed. "If they'd just go out in the desert and kill each other, it might not be so bad. It won't happen that way, though. If that feud starts up again in earnest, a lot of innocent folks are going to get hurt." Chadwell went to the door. "Well, thanks, Doc."

The doctor muttered a farewell, and Chadwell went back out into the early afternoon heat.

He walked down the street to the courthouse and gratefully entered the coolness retained by the thick walls. Ike Ring was just coming out of the cellblock when Chadwell entered the office.

" 'Lo, Billy," Ring grunted. "What can I do for you?"

"I'd like to talk to Matt Lindsay as soon as he wakes up," Chadwell said. "That all right with you?"

"Evan Maddock's not with you, is he?"

"No. He rode back out to his ranch with Ted and Nacho," Chadwell told the sheriff.

"In that case, you can talk to Matt. Not sure why you want to, though."

Chadwell turned a straight-backed chair around and straddled it as Ring sat down behind the desk. "I'm not sure, either," he admitted. "I've got a feeling that there's more to the story than what we've heard so far, though, and I've learned to trust my hunches."

"If you can get any more out of Matt than I did, I'll be surprised. The boy must've been drunk as a skunk last night."

"Well, we'll see," Chadwell said thoughtfully. "You think there's going to be trouble when Axel and Jubal hear about this, Ike?"

"Bound to be," Ring said, his face and voice gloomy. "Lord, but I hate a bunch of trouble in my town, especially shootin' trouble."

"Maybe it won't come to that."

"Yeah, maybe." Ring sounded doubtful.

The two men talked for half an hour, comfortable with each other's company as they discussed the problems that had descended on Pecos.

Ring had leaned back in his chair and settled his boots on the desk, but the legs of his chair came down with an abrupt thump as a weak call of "Sheriff! Hey, Sheriff!" came from the cellblock.

"Sounds like Matt's awake again," Ring said as he stood up. "He's the only one back there right now. Come on, Billy."

Chadwell followed as Ring unlocked the cellblock door. They went down a wide aisle between the cells. Matt was in the middle cell on the right, stretched out on the cot suspended from the thick stone wall. His shoulder was heavily bandaged, and his left arm was strapped to his side so that he couldn't move it.

He raised up slightly on his right elbow as Ring and Chadwell came to the door of the cell. He appeared totally sober now, but he was pale and obviously very weak.

"What can I do for you, Matt?" Ring asked.

Matt licked dry lips. "I'd sure appreciate something to drink, Sheriff."

"You know there's no liquor allowed in jail, Matt," the sheriff told him sternly.

"Hell, right now I'd even drink water." Matt slitted his eyes and peered in the shadowy dimness at the man with Ring. "Who's that?"

"It's Billy Chadwell, Matt," the lawyer said as he stepped closer to the cell. "I'd like to talk to you."

"I'll get that water for you, Matt," Ring said, turning back toward the office.

"I don't understand," Matt said slowly as he stared at Chadwell. "You're Evan Maddock's partner. What do you want with me?"

Chadwell leaned against the bars of the cell. "I may be Evan's partner," he said, "but first and foremost I'm an officer of the court, and finding out the truth is my duty. Did you know you're going to be charged with murder, Matt?"

"Murder?" Matt frowned and carefully shook his aching head. "I remember something about Johnny Maddock bein' dead. Are they sayin' I did it?"

"That's what it looks like. Both of you were found on the trail to the Maddock ranch. It appeared that you had shot it out. Don't you remember that?"

"No, sir, I don't," Matt said firmly. "But to tell you the truth, I don't remember much of anything after I started drinkin' in the Double Eagle."

"You don't remember leaving the saloon, riding out of town?"

Matt shook his head. "No, sir, I don't."

"It sounds to me like when the trial comes up you're not going to have much of a defense." Chadwell looked intently at Matt's face for a moment and saw nothing there but confusion and pain. Abruptly, he made a decision on an idea that had been nagging at him all afternoon. "But you're going to need a lawyer anyway. In your case, a damn good lawyer. Like me."

Matt's eyes widened. He couldn't believe what he

was hearing. "You're offerin' to take my case?" he asked. "But Evan Maddock's your partner."

"That doesn't matter. If you accept, Evan won't be handling your case, I will. How about it, Matt?"

"No tricks?" Matt squinted suspiciously at him.

"No tricks," Chadwell assured him.

After a moment, Matt sighed in resignation. "I'm in trouble, all right. Don't know why you're doin' this, Mr. Chadwell, but if you're willin' to help me, I'm willin' to take it."

"Good!" Chadwell exclaimed. He knew that many people would question the wisdom of his taking on this case, but he felt that he had done the right thing.

Sheriff Ring came back into the cellblock. He was carrying a cup of water, and he was cursing.

"We got trouble," he snapped as he unlocked the cell door, stepped through, and handed the cup to Matt. Just as quickly, he was back out, relocking the door. "You'd better get out of here while you've got the chance, Billy. I just got word that the Maddocks and the Lindsays are ridin' into town. Figure they'll meet up right outside in a few minutes."

Matt raised himself higher on his good elbow and grinned broadly, some of his arrogance coming back. "My daddy's come to get me out," he said triumphantly. "He ain't gonna let me rot in jail."

"Like hell he'll take you out of here," Ring bristled. "I'm duly charged with the safekeepin' of prisoners, and that means you ain't goin' anywhere until I say so!"

"Busting out of here won't do you any good, Matt," Chadwell added. "You'd have a murder charge hanging over your head the rest of your life. You'd have to stay on the run all the time. The only thing that'll really help you is beating the charge in court."

"I'd best get outside," Ring said. "You comin' or not, Billy?"

"I'll stay," Chadwell replied quietly.

"All right. But come out in the office so that I can lock the cellblock door."

"I'll be back to talk to you, Matt," Chadwell promised and then followed Ring out into the office.

There was shouting in the street outside. Ring took down a double-barreled shotgun from the rack on the wall, broke it open, checked the loads, and then stepped to the door. "Stay back, Billy," he warned.

"I'm not about to get in the way," Chadwell said.

Ring strode out onto the little porch just outside his office. Two stone steps led down to the patchy lawn that surrounded the courthouse. Ring stopped at the bottom of the steps and stood ready, the shotgun cradled in his arms.

Chadwell stepped into the doorway and caught his breath at the spectacle outside. The Maddocks and the Lindsays had arrived. Silence was settling over the city now, as people ducked for cover.

Axel Maddock and his men sat their horses on the south side of the courthouse square, facing across the grassy area to where Jubal Lindsay and his men waited on the north side.

There were over a dozen riders in each group, and guns were in evidence everywhere. Winchesters were ready in callused hands, and Colts rode loose in their holsters. Axel Maddock was holding a Winchester, and it was no accident that its muzzle was pointing toward Jubal Lindsay.

"Here, now!" Sheriff Ike Ring called. "What do you men want?"

Axel and Jubal were staring at each other, and they didn't tear their gazes loose as Jubal spat out the side of his mouth and said, "I come to get my boy out of jail, Sheriff."

"And I come to see that justice is done," Axel shot back in reply. "We aim to give Matt a fair trial and a fair hangin'."

"There'll be no hangin' in Pecos while I'm sheriff!" Ring shouted. "Not until a judge orders one. Axel, Jubal, I think you and your men had best go home. Everything's under control here and'll be done accordin' to law."

"No law says you can hang my boy for killin' a snake," Jubal Lindsay growled.

"Killin' a snake!" Axel howled. "Why, there was never a Lindsay born fit to lick the boots of a Maddock, you pig-faced old horse thief!"

"Horse thief, is it?" Jubal's hand started toward his Colt, and the Winchester snapped up to the ready in Axel's gnarled fingers.

"Hold it!" Ring ordered. He lined the barrels of the shotgun on Jubal Lindsay. "If you two old buzzards don't settle down, I'll blast both of you! One barrel for you, Jubal, and the second one for you, Axel!"

"You'd never make it, Ike," Axel sneered. "You might drop that skunk over there, but my boys'll fill you full of lead 'fore you could turn this way."

Ring grinned. "Is that so, Axel? Your hands might not mind tradin' shots with the Lindsays, but you really think they'll shoot down an officer of the law who's just doin' his duty?"

There was a shuffling of discomfort among the Maddock riders, and the group headed by Jubal Lindsay didn't look too happy with the idea of firing on Sheriff Ring, either.

It was a standoff, and everyone knew it. Either the two patriarchs would back off . . . or the courthouse square would become a bloody battleground.

A block away, Howell Trainor, his daughter Kathy, and Warren Prescott watched from the window of their hotel suite. Trainor and Prescott had returned to the hotel following their meeting with the sheriff and the district attorney. As soon as her father told her about the turn of events that had caused him to take on the responsibility of prosecuting Matt Lindsay, she had thought it was a mistake. Now she was sure of it.

Getting involved in this case just might cause Howell Trainor to wind up dead.

The same thought had occurred to the senator as he watched the confrontation between the two warring families. Perhaps he had taken on too much; the risk might be too great, even though his involvement in the case was sure to net him a great deal of publicity.

Warren Prescott suppressed the eagerness and excitement he felt as he waited to see if war would erupt on the streets of Pecos. He and Trainor had already been to the telegraph office to get in touch with the attorney general in Austin, and by now word would be getting around about Trainor's involvement with the case. By tomorrow, newspapers in Fort Worth, Dallas, San Antonio, Houston, and El Paso would be getting ready to send reporters to cover the trial.

So far, Prescott was more than satisfied with the outcome of his plan.

There were others watching the confrontation in the street between the Maddocks and the Lindsays. The whole town was holding its breath. Just inside the doorway of the Orient Saloon, Cal Ahern stood with Celestina. She was wearing a fancy silk dress he had bought for her early in his stay in Pecos, before his money had run so low. They had been out for a walk—Ahern had to admit that both of them enjoyed the scandalized looks the respectable ladies of the city gave them—when the potentially violent situation in the square had developed. The Orient was the closest place to duck into for protection against any bullets that might start flying.

Ahern was watching the confrontation intently, and there was a worried frown on his face. Celestina, looking up at his face, saw in his disturbed expression more than just concern that they might be caught in some stray gunfire. His arm was around her, and she huddled closer against him.

"What is wrong, Cal?" she asked quietly.

He shook his head, never taking his eyes off the scene. "Nothing," he said absentmindedly.

Celestina bit her lip and said nothing more. There were times when it was impossible to get through to Cal, and this seemed to be one of them.

The Orient's patrons stood at the windows of the saloon, anxious to see what would happen next. They regarded the situation with mixed emotions. Day-to-day life could be deadly dull, and an outbreak of fighting between the Maddocks and the Lindsays would definitely spice things up. But at the same time, a city caught in the middle could go up in flames if the violence got carried away.

Billy Chadwell was thinking the same thing as he stood on the little porch outside the sheriff's office. Somebody had to do something to pull the fuse on this powder keg.

He went down the steps, pushed past Sheriff Ring, and walked out onto the grass between the two armed groups. Ring hissed, "Billy, what the hell you doin'?"

Chadwell ignored him. He stopped midway between Axel Maddock and Jubal Lindsay and looked from one to the other, his face taut and angry.

"I swear, if you two aren't the stubbornest old goats I've ever seen!" he said, raising his voice so that everyone in the vicinity of the square could hear him. "You ought to be ashamed of yourselves, coming in here and threatening to take the law into your own hands!"

"You stay out of this, Billy," Axel Maddock warned. "You may be Evan's partner, but that don't give you the right to stick your nose in our business."

"Good way to get your nose shot off," Jubal Lindsay added with a growl.

From the side, Ike Ring raised his shotgun and called, "Get the hell out of there, Billy!"

Chadwell shook his head. "No, sir. I can be stubborn, too, and I'm not going to let you two old goats shoot up this city. Why don't you just go on home? The truth'll come out at the trial."

"Ain't gonna be no trial," Jubal snapped.

"But there sure as hell's goin' to be a hangin'!" Axel added.

"There *is* going to be a trial, a fair and legal one," Chadwell insisted. "I know because I'm going to represent Matt as his legal counsel."

It was a toss-up as to who looked more stunned by this announcement—Axel Maddock, Jubal Lindsay, or Ike Ring.

Axel broke the shocked silence first. "You can't do that!" he exclaimed. "Evan's your partner. You can't stab him in the back that way!"

"If Evan feels that I'm betraying him, he's free to leave the firm," Chadwell said calmly.

"You can't be the boy's lawyer," Jubal Lindsay burst out. "You'll sell him up the river! Everybody knows you and Evan been friends a long time."

Chadwell met Jubal's red-rimmed gaze. "You've known me a lot of years, Jubal," he said. "Am I an honest man?"

Jubal spat again, considered, and said, "Reckon you are."

"I give you my word that I'll do my best for Matt." Chadwell's face broke out in a cocky grin. "And do you know of a better lawyer around here than me?"

Jubal glared, but said, "Reckon not."

"There." Chadwell brushed off his hands. "Everybody ought to be satisfied for the moment. Matt will stand trial, and a judge and jury will decide what's fair and proper. You boys go on home."

There was a long moment of silence, and then Axel Maddock raised the Winchester and shook it at Chadwell. "We'll go . . . for now. But I promise you this much, Billy: If the law don't work the way it should, we'll be back to take care of it ourselves. Either way, Matt Lindsay is goin' to hang!"

"Well, I've got a promise to make, too," Jubal called out. "If my boy hangs because of some phony murder charge, I'll see that the score is settled. Settled with blood!"

Slowly, both groups of riders began to back their horses away from the square. Then they wheeled their mounts around, dug in their spurs, and galloped away.

For the time being, Pecos was safe.

But the message of this confrontation was plain. Whichever way the trial turned out, one family wasn't going to be satisfied. And that meant open, total warfare—unless somebody could come up with an answer that would pacify both groups.

A pretty tall order, Chadwell thought as he turned

and walked back to the sheriff's office. He was still grinning, but a fine sheen of sweat on his forehead showed just how much of a strain he had really been under.

Ike Ring rested the shotgun on his shoulder and gazed in wonderment at Chadwell. "You are the craziest son of a bitch I ever saw," he said fervently.

Chadwell nodded. "I know," he said.

Chapter Nine

The sunset was magnificent, casting an orange-red glow over the rolling plains as the sun sank behind the rugged mountains in the distance. It was a pretty sight, all right. But Evan Maddock was in no mood to appreciate it as he leaned on the railing of the veranda that ran all the way around the ranch house.

The afternoon had been a painful blur. He barely remembered the ride out here from town. Ted had retreated to his room as soon as they arrived, and Evan had wandered through the rest of the house, letting the memories wash over him as he kept seeing things that reminded him of Johnny.

It did no good to tell himself that death was a natural part of life, that grief was a part of the human condition just as surely as was happiness.

Johnny had been cut down before hardly having a chance to live; his death was totally unnatural, totally unfair. And the grieving hurt like hell.

At some point Evan became aware that he hadn't eaten since morning. Starving himself wasn't going to make things any better, and he realized it was likely that Ted hadn't eaten since morning, either. So he had gone to the kitchen and told the old Chinese cook to prepare dinner.

By the time the meal was ready, Evan had lost his appetite again, but he forced himself to eat, so that maybe Ted would eat, too. Ted proved to be no problem, though; he came out of his room when Evan called him, and he ate well, if silently. In fact, he had said very little since they had come back to the ranch, and Evan was starting to worry that the boy was *too* quiet. He was holding too much inside, not letting out the pain and the anger.

After dinner, Evan went outside and stood on the veranda. Leaning on the railing and staring out into the twilight, he realized that he was doing the same thing as Ted—holding in too much pain.

He heard the screen door open and close behind him, and Nacho Newcomb said, "How you makin' it, amigo?"

Evan turned around and rested his hip against the rail. "I'm all right," he said. "Where's Ted?"

"Went back to his room. I think he's asleep." Nacho lowered his bulk into a rocking chair on the veranda and started rolling a cigarette. "Nice night tonight."

Evan heard the faraway song of a bird serenading the end of the day. There were faint noises coming from the barn as some of the hands went about their final chores. The sun had disappeared behind the mountains now, and shadows were falling quickly over the ranch. There was a slight breeze out of the west, relieving the heat and bringing a hint of coolness to the dusk.

"Yes," Evan said. "A nice night."

Nacho looked off to the north and said, "Somebody's coming."

Evan followed the big foreman's gaze and saw a buggy rolling down the trail from Pecos. He recognized the stout figure of Billy Chadwell in the box.

A few minutes later, Chadwell brought the horse to a stop in front of the house and climbed down from the buggy. He stepped up onto the porch and said, "Hello, Evan. Evening, Nacho." Evan thought Chadwell looked tired and drawn, but that could have been a trick of the falling light.

"Hello, Billy," Evan replied. "Have a seat."

"Don't mind if I do." Chadwell sank gratefully into the other rocking chair next to Nacho. He asked, "How's Ted?"

"Bearing up, just like the rest of us." Evan kept his worries about the boy to himself. "How are things in town?"

Chadwell took a pipe and a pouch of tobacco from the

pocket of his coat and answered as he began to pack the bowl. "We almost had quite a little shindig this afternoon. Your uncle Axel came into town with his men when he heard about Johnny—came to get Matt Lindsay. They got there at the same time as old Jubal and his riders. It got a little tense there in the square."

Nacho muttered an exclamation in Spanish at Chadwell's understated comment.

"Anybody get hurt?" Evan asked anxiously.

Chadwell shook his head. "There was no shooting, just a lot of threatening. Ike Ring had already moved Matt over to the jail from Doc's office, and he met them outside with a shotgun. It was a near thing, but we were able to convince Axel and Jubal to let the law handle it."

"We?"

"I knew I wouldn't be able to slip that one by you," Chadwell said with a grin. His face sobered as he went on, "I told them I was going to represent Matt at his trial."

Evan stiffened, straightening from his leaning position against the railing. He felt as though someone had just punched him in the belly.

"You told them *what*?"

"You heard me, son. Matt and I agreed that I would handle his defense."

Nacho stared at Chadwell and flicked his cigarette out into the sand in front of the porch. "You're Evan's friend, Mr. Chadwell," he said flatly. "That's the only reason I'm not throwing you off this ranch right now."

"I don't believe you, Billy," Evan said. "You couldn't defend a no-good murdering bas—"

"Why?" Chadwell cut in sharply. "Why is he a no-good murdering bastard? Because he's a Lindsay? One of the fundamental rights of this country is that everyone is entitled to a defense in court, no matter what his last name is."

"He killed my brother, dammit!"

"Did he?" Chadwell shot back quickly. "A man's innocent until *proven* guilty, Evan. You know that."

"What more proof could you want? You know how I found the two of them!" Evan knew his voice was rising with anger, and he was afraid that Ted might hear him, but he couldn't help it. He had thought that he knew Billy Chadwell. . . .

"I know how it looked," Chadwell admitted. "Maybe Matt *is* guilty. But he still deserves the best defense he can get, and I *am* the best lawyer in this part of the country."

"I used to think so," Evan snapped in a voice tinged with bitterness.

Chadwell stood up and faced Evan. He was starting to get angry now, too. "Dammit, Evan," he snapped, "something's not right with this case, and I'm going to find out what it is."

"What do you mean?"

"I mean it's not as simple as it looks." Chadwell started to pace up and down the veranda. "Something else is going on that we can't see just yet."

"What you are saying makes no sense," Nacho said. He hauled himself up out of the chair. "You're talking like you think Lindsay didn't shoot Johnny."

"Maybe he didn't," Chadwell said. "Look at it this way, both of you: If Matt did shoot Johnny, why doesn't he just claim that Johnny shot first and that he fired back in self-defense? No one could dispute that story. But what does Matt do instead? He claims that he can't remember what happened. Why would he say something that he knows can't help him, unless it's the truth?"

"Maybe he just didn't think fast enough when the sheriff was questioning him," Evan objected. "After all, he had been shot, and he was in a lot of pain."

"I talked to him later, in the jail, and he stuck to his story." Chadwell reached out and put a hand on his partner's arm. "I believe him, Evan. I believe he honestly doesn't know what happened last night."

"That still doesn't make him innocent, just because he doesn't remember shooting Johnny."

"You're right, it doesn't make him innocent. But it creates enough doubt to make a trial a necessity. Lynching Matt doesn't get us any answers."

Evan sighed. "You're right about that much. I don't want him lynched."

"It'd be understandable if you did," Chadwell said gently.

"*Sí*, I almost cut the bastard's throat myself," Nacho added. "I'm still not sure I should not have."

Evan clenched his right hand into a fist and drove it into the palm of his left one. "I just want the truth now," he said. "I want to know what happened out there beside the trail."

"That's what we all want." Chadwell hesitated and then said, "That's why I want you to help me with this case, Evan."

Another oath exploded from Nacho as Even stared in disbelief at Chadwell. "You want me to help defend my brother's killer?"

"I want you to help me find the truth. You're the best I've ever seen at digging out facts, Evan. Work as my investigator; stay behind the scenes. I'll handle the trial." He saw the dubious look on Evan's face and added, "After all, we're both after the truth."

Chadwell's plea had come as a complete surprise to Evan, and everything in him rebelled at the very idea of doing something to help the defense of Matt Lindsay.

But there was no denying the sincerity in Chadwell's voice when he spoke of believing Matt's story. By basing his request on a search for the truth, Chadwell had put Evan in a position where it was hard to turn him down.

"All right," he said finally, surprising both himself and Nacho. "I'll do it. But I'll help you for one reason, Billy, and one reason alone. I'm not working for Lindsay, Billy; I'm working for the truth. I intend to find out what happened, and if I turn up any solid evidence that Matt is guilty, I'm going right to Howell Trainor with it."

Chadwell grinned. "Fair enough."

Evan shook his head. Everything was going too fast. This morning he hadn't even known that Johnny was dead; now he practically was working for the defense of the man accused of killing Johnny. The law could be a strange thing sometimes. But he had to abide by it and trust that it would bring the real killer to justice.

"Speaking of Trainor," Evan said, more to take his mind off what had just happened than anything else, "how do you feel about going up against a high-powered opponent like him?"

Chadwell's smile widened in anticipation. "I'm looking forward to it," he said quickly. "He may find out that us old country lawyers aren't as slow as he thinks."

Looking at Chadwell, Evan had to agree. Howell Trainor was in for a fight.

In a hotel room in Pecos, another meeting that could help determine the fate of Matt Lindsay was about to take place.

Warren Prescott answered a soft knock on his door and opened it to find Cal Ahern standing there in the hall. Without preamble, Ahern said urgently. "I've got to talk to you, Prescott."

Prescott grimaced, took Ahern's arm, and hustled him into the room, quickly shutting the door behind him. The door of the Trainor suite was shut, and Prescott was grateful for that much.

"What the hell are you doing here?" he hissed at Ahern. "I told you I didn't want the senator to see us together."

"He didn't see me."

"How did you know where to find me?"

"An important man like you isn't hard to find." Ahern passed a shaking hand over his face. There were beads of perspiration on his upper lip. He was clearly a very frightened man. "Did you see what happened this afternoon when the Maddocks and the Lindsays rode in? Dammit, Prescott, I've got to get out of town!"

Prescott stared at the gambler, cold contempt in his eyes. "Nothing happened this afternoon," he said flatly. "A couple of old banty roosters tried to make themselves look tough."

"You just don't know how close it came to a shooting scrape."

"I know this much," Prescott told him. "Leaving town right now is probably the worst thing you could do. That would just draw attention to you, and people might start to remember that you had a grudge against Johnny Maddock, too."

"He owed me some money—"

"And he outdrew you and made you look like a fool in the Flores Cantina," Prescott said savagely. "You wanted him dead, and you know it."

More sweat appeared on Ahern's face. "You know what'll happen to me if anybody finds out that I'm the one who really shot Maddock and Lindsay? My life won't be worth a goddamned penny!"

Prescott took a deep breath and went to the dressing table. A carafe of brandy sat there, brought up earlier from the hotel bar. There were also several glasses. He filled one of them with liquor and carried it over to Ahern.

"Perhaps this will calm your nerves," he said.

"My nerves are calm enough. It's my gut that's afraid I'm going to wind up dead. Just because I listened to you," Ahern added bitterly.

When Ahern wouldn't take the brandy, Prescott shrugged and sipped it himself. "Listen to me," he said. "Matt Lindsay is going to be tried for killing Johnny Maddock, just as I planned. No one knows you had anything to do with it if you carried out the plan the way I explained it to you."

Ahern took a deep breath. "I did. I did everything like you said. I waylaid Matt when he left the Double Eagle and knocked him out and then took him out to the trail. I tied him up and left him there and then came back to town to follow Johnny out. I even took Matt's gun with me and used it on Johnny. Then I used Johnny's gun to wound Matt after I untied him. It all went just the way you figured."

"And we both got the results we wanted. Johnny Maddock is dead, and Senator Trainor will reap enough publicity from the trial to assure his election. *And* I paid you double what Maddock owed you."

"It's not enough," Ahern muttered, looking down at the floor.

"What did you say?"

"I said it's not enough." Ahern raised his eyes and looked truculently at Prescott. "If I'm going to run the risk of staying around here, I've got to have more money."

Prescott sighed. Almost from the moment he had opened the door and found Ahern standing there, he had anticipated just such a demand. "How much?" he asked.

"Another couple of hundred ought to do it."

Prescott nodded. "All right." He took a wallet from the inside pocket of his coat and counted out several bills. Pressing them into Ahern's outstretched hand, he said, "I expect you to keep holding up your end of the bargain, though. Don't make any trouble that will draw attention to you. As far as you're concerned, you have no connection with this case, and you should act accordingly."

"Right." Ahern seemed calmer now that he had the money. He gave Prescott a sly smile. "After all, we're in this together, aren't we? If I'm not safe, you're not safe."

"I suppose that's right," Prescott said impatiently. *My God, what a crude specimen I've chosen*, he thought. Ahern couldn't have couched his blackmail innuendos any more blatantly.

"I'd better get back to the cantina before Celestina starts to worry about me," Ahern said, starting toward the door.

Prescott got in front of him, opened the door slightly, and checked the hallway before swinging the door back for the gambler to exit. "That's a good idea," he said. "Just keep your wits about you, and everything will be all right."

"Sure. Good night."

Prescott waited until Ahern had turned the corner at the head of the stairs and then closed his door. Inside, he was seething. He became aware that he still had the half-full glass of brandy in his hand, and he swallowed the rest of the liquor in one gulp.

Prescott had faith in his plan, even though it had been conceived hastily and on the spur of the moment.

You had to believe in yourself, or there was no point in daring the odds and reaching for your goals.

But in this case, he also had to depend on Cal Ahern, and Ahern gave every indication that he might turn out to be a liability rather than an asset.

In that case, Warren Prescott knew, his course was a simple one. Whenever possible, liabilities had to be removed.

Chapter Ten

When Evan opened his eyes the next morning, at first he didn't remember what had happened the day before. All his sleep-drugged mind knew was that he was in his old room at the ranch house, rather than in the room he rented in Pecos. There were clean sheets on the bed, and they felt good as he stretched his long legs. A shaft of sunlight slanted into the room from the open window. Evan yawned.

Then he sat bolt upright as the realization hit him that this was the morning they were going to bury his brother.

Dazed, he dressed and went downstairs to breakfast. Ted was there at the table, but he was still uncommunicative. As the two brothers were finishing breakfast, Nacho came in through the back door, wearing his Sunday clothes, the fabric of his suit stretched tightly over his massive frame.

"The wagon is ready," he said quietly.

Nacho drove the team. Evan and Ted sat beside him in the box, and behind the wagon the Maddock hands rode solemnly. As the procession approached the small family cemetery at the crest of a rolling hill, Evan saw that a large crowd was already gathered there.

Axel Maddock was in attendance, along with his wife, Reba, and their daughters-in-law, the women all dressed in the severe black dresses they had worn to the last Maddock funeral—when sons and husbands had been buried.

A sizable contingent of townspeople had made the drive out from Pecos, among them Billy Chadwell. Kathy and Howell Trainor were also there, along with Warren Prescott. Evan's eyes met Kathy's for a moment, and he saw genuine compassion there.

Evan climbed down from the wagon as Nacho brought it to a halt. Then he made his way through the crowd to Billy's side, pausing to shake several hands along the way and listen to murmured condolences.

"Thanks for being here, Billy," Evan said quietly as he came up to the older lawyer.

Chadwell made no reply other than to reach out to squeeze Evan's arm.

Ted and Nacho came up to join Evan in the front rank of mourners. They stared at the coffin of fine hardwood, polished to a high sheen and decorated with elaborate scrollwork on the lid.

Evan thought he had never seen an uglier sight.

He hardly heard what the preacher had to say. The service seemed to take forever, and when it was finally over, the crowd scattered quickly, most of the mourners only too happy to leave behind this scene pervaded with the dark presence of death. The sun was shining altogether too brightly for a funeral.

And along with the grief in the air was an undeniable sense of anger. A Maddock was dead, and someone should be made to pay.

Evan put his hat on and walked away from the gravesite as the undertaker's men began to fill it in. His hand was on Ted's shoulder, and he maintained a firm grip, leading the boy away. Nacho and Billy Chadwell fell into step beside them.

"I'll be into town in a little while, Billy," Evan said tonelessly. "There'll be a lot of work to do."

"It doesn't have to be today, Evan," Chadwell said.

"Yes, it does," Evan told him. "The truth won't wait. I won't wait."

"All right. I'll see you later." Chadwell veered off from the little group and went back to his buggy.

Evan reached up and yanked his tie loose, something that Ted and Nacho had already done. He didn't feel like wearing a suit today. "I've got to change clothes," he said.

"Sí," Nacho agreed, running a finger around the tight collar of his shirt.

"How about you, Ted?" Evan asked.

"Johnny never liked wearin' no monkey suit," Ted replied sullenly. He walked faster, shrugging his shoulder out from under Evan's hand.

Evan and Nacho exchanged a helpless look and followed Ted back to the wagon.

By the time Evan came down from his room a bit later wearing boots, jeans, and a work shirt, Ted was nowhere to be seen in the house. Evan didn't want to ride into Pecos without saying good-bye to him; part of his mind told him that he shouldn't leave the ranch at all today, that he needed to stay here with Ted. But Ted didn't seem to want his company, and he might be able to do something more useful in Pecos with Billy Chadwell.

He stepped out onto the porch, looking for Ted, and spotted the boy sitting in one of the rocking chairs.

There was a Winchester lying on the porch beside him, and Ted held a Colt in his hand. As Evan watched, he put down the cleaning rag he had been using on it and started taking cartridges from the shell belt he wore around his waist. He thumbed the bullets into the cylinder of the gun with practiced ease.

"What the blue blazes are you doing, Ted?" Evan demanded, the words out of his mouth before he could recall them. The presence of the rifle didn't surprise him; everyone carried a Winchester if they did much riding. But he hadn't known that Ted even owned a six-gun, much less a well-oiled holster for it.

Ted looked up at him, the cold eyes of a man peering out from that boyish face and making a shiver run down Evan's spine.

"What does it look like I'm doing? With so many Lindsay men around, a man's got to go armed."

Evan held his tongue about Ted not even being a man yet, figuring that such a comment would only make the situation worse. Instead, he asked, "Where did you get the Colt?"

That was a mistake, too. "From Johnny," Ted replied,

his voice flat but his face bleak. "And if I run into any Lindsays, I intend to shoot first. They're not going to get me."

Evan's heart went out to Ted; he knew the kind of pain and anger the boy must be feeling. But at the same time, Evan was angry, too—angry that Ted would take this approach to the problem.

"That was the kind of attitude Johnny had. Look what happened to him." Evan knew the words were harsh, perhaps even cruel, but he felt as if he had to get through to Ted before he did something they would all regret.

"It won't happen to me," Ted insisted. He slipped the gun into its holster. "Johnny taught me a lot. I'll keep practicing. I'll be ready when the time comes."

"If you go looking for trouble, that time could be sooner than you think."

Ted stood up and turned his back. "My brother is dead," he said without looking at Evan. "There's a score that's got to be settled. I don't see *you* doing anything about it."

The sharp words cut into Evan. He hadn't told Ted that he was doing investigative work that might end up assisting Matt Lindsay's defense. His words to Chadwell at the cemetery had been purposely vague, so that Ted wouldn't find out about this latest development. There was no way Ted could understand, especially not now. Evan still wasn't sure he completely understood himself.

Ted would find out eventually, Evan realized. But not now, not yet.

He looked at Ted's stiff, unyielding back for a moment and then left the porch and strode toward the barn. There was nothing else he could do.

Nacho was in the barn when Evan went in to saddle his horse. Evan jerked his head toward the house and said, "Ted's got a gun."

"I know," Nacho said with a sigh. "I saw him with it earlier. This is a bad thing, Evan, a very bad thing."

"Maybe we can keep it from getting any worse," Evan replied as he led his horse from its stall. "Can you keep an eye on him, Nacho? He's got a lot of crazy ideas in his head right now, but he's smart enough. I think he'll settle down if we can just ride herd on him for a while."

Nacho nodded. "Sí. I'll watch him. I'll put him to work, that's what I'll do. Not much trouble you can get into when you're worn out from mending fences."

"Good idea," Evan agreed. He saddled up rapidly. Knowing that he could depend on Nacho Newcomb made it a little easier to leave the ranch and go back to Pecos.

He pushed the horse into a gallop once he was on the trail. As he rode past the place where he had found Johnny and Matt, he couldn't help but relive the scene in his mind. The hurt was as painful as ever. Time would be needed to heal that wound, plenty of time.

Chadwell was waiting at the law office, idly flipping through one of the heavy legal volumes. Evan came in, hung his hat on a peg, and sat down across the table from Chadwell.

"All right," he said bluntly, "where do we start?"

Chadwell shut the law book with a solid thump. "We start by approaching the case like it was any other case. I know that's going to be hard, but we've got to do it. Objectivity is one of the strongest weapons we have."

"Whatever you say, Billy. You're in charge."

"Good. Let's start by going over the facts we know."

Chadwell was right about one thing, Evan thought several times in the next hour—being objective about this case was going to be next to impossible. But he forced his mind to stay as cool and collected as possible as he and Chadwell discussed everything they knew about the events of the previous morning and the night before that.

Finally, Evan shook his head and said, "I just don't see what kind of defense you can offer for Matt, Billy. You can't even afford to put him on the witness stand to testify for himself."

"Oh? Why not?" Chadwell knew the answer to that one quite well, but he wanted to see if Evan had followed the same mental process.

"He's already said several times that he doesn't know what happened, that he doesn't remember. If he tells another story now, even if it's true he's going to sound like he made it up to try to save his skin."

"That's right."

"Anyway," Evan went on, "I still think he's guilty. I still think he followed Johnny and fired first. Are you sure you want me handling the investigation when I feel like that?"

Chadwell clasped his hands together on the table and leaned forward. "The way I see it, our only real defense is to find out what really happened out there—and who really killed Johnny if Matt didn't. Your job is to dig around and find out; mine is to stall long enough to give you a chance. To speak frankly, Evan, Matt Lindsay's life is in your hands. I feel comfortable about that only because I know you want this town to see that the law can be counted on, even in a case with so many heated emotions. To answer your question—there's no one in the world I'd rather have working with me on this one."

Evan nodded slowly. "All right. I suppose I can't argue with that."

"I hope not." Chadwell stood up and went to get his hat. "Come on. Let's go talk to Matt."

Evan had been dreading this meeting, though he had known that it would come sooner or later. He got his hat and followed Chadwell out of the office.

Sheriff Ring wasn't at the jail when they arrived, but Deputy Lew Lansdale was and had been given orders by Ring to let the two attorneys see the prisoner.

"Doc's back there with him now," Lansdale said as he unlocked the cellblock door. "I'll see if he's through."

Lansdale and the doctor came out a moment later, the doctor carrying his black bag. "Don't wear him out," he warned Evan and Chadwell. "He's better today, but he's still weak."

"We'll be careful, Doc," Chadwell promised.

Matt was sitting up today, and when he saw Evan, he came to his feet, his face turning belligerent. "What the hell are you doing here, Maddock?" he demanded.

Chadwell moved between the two of them and held

up his hands. "Now, Matt, don't jump to any conclusions. Evan has agreed to help me prepare your case."

"Help you?" Matt snorted. "The only thing he'd like to prepare for me is the gallows!"

Evan took a deep breath and held onto his temper. "Billy's telling the truth, Matt. I don't like you, but I'm willing to help find out the truth. If you are innocent, I certainly don't want to see you hang."

Matt sat down on his cot, lifted his good hand, and rubbed the back of his neck. "Reckon I appreciate that, Evan. Guess I'm just snappish 'cause my head hurts so much. I picked up a pretty good bump somewhere."

There was a three-legged stool sitting in front of one of the other cells. Chadwell drew it over to him with a foot and sat down while Evan stood beside him. "I know we've been over this before, Matt," Chadwell began, "but I'd like you to tell us again everything you remember about the night before last."

Just as riding along the trail between Pecos and the ranch had been painful for Evan, so, too, was listening to Matt talk about Johnny and their confrontation in the cantina. He began by saying, "I'd been out back with one of the gals, and when we come back in Johnny was standing there at the bar, laughing and joking. I'd had plenty to drink myself, and I figured it'd be a good time to see how fast he was."

Matt went on to detail how Flores had stopped the showdown almost before it started. Then he told Evan and Chadwell as much as he remembered about the rest of the evening, which wasn't much once he reached the Double Eagle Saloon and started pouring more whiskey into his belly.

The two attorneys spent an hour with their client, and then Chadwell sighed and stood up. "Can't keep on plowing the same piece of ground, I guess," he said. "We'll think on things and be back to see you later, Matt."

"All right. Evan . . . thanks."

"For what?" Evan asked. "I haven't done anything yet."

Matt summoned up a grin. "You didn't come gunning for me. That's something."

Evan smiled thinly. "Suppose you're right."

He and Chadwell left the jail after nodding a farewell to Deputy Lansdale. The sheriff still hadn't returned.

They hadn't been gone more than a minute when the door of the sheriff's office opened again and a man in range clothes stuck his head inside. Lansdale looked up from the copy of the *Police Gazette* he had spread out on the desk and recognized the man as one of the hands who rode for Axel Maddock.

"Say, weren't that Evan Maddock who just come out'a here?" the hand asked.

"That's right," Lansdale said. "Him and Chadwell were back talking to their client."

"You mean Evan's working for Matt Lindsay?"

"That's what Ike—I mean Sheriff Ring—told me," Lansdale confirmed.

The hand's jaw was slack with surprise. "I'll be jiggered," he muttered and then ducked back out of the door and closed it with a slam.

Lansdale shook his head and muttered, "Cowboys," conveniently forgetting that he had been a cowhand himself until Ike Ring had hired him less than a year earlier.

Outside, the Maddock hand hurried to the hitching rack where his horse was tied up. A minute later, he was spurring out of town at a fast gallop.

Evan and Chadwell were taking their time about walking back to the office. Chadwell said thoughtfully, "The way I see it, we've got four possibilities in this case, Evan."

"How do you figure that?"

Chadwell held up his hand and ticked off each theory on a pudgy finger. "One, somebody unknown ambushed Johnny and killed him, and then Matt happened to come along just at the wrong time and got shot when he stumbled on the real killer."

"Guess it could have happened that way," Evan admitted.

"Two, just the opposite of that situation could have

occurred, which would mean that the killer was really after Matt and that Johnny was an unlucky bystander."

"If that was the case, why didn't the killer finish off Matt?"

Chadwell shrugged. "Maybe he got scared after Johnny showed up and he had to shoot him. It's hard to know just what a killer will do. His actions won't always make sense." Chadwell paused and then said, "The third possibility is that everything happened just like you think it did, Evan. I could be wrong about Matt. If I am, I'm sorry I dragged you into this."

"You're doing what you think is right, aren't you?"

"Yes," Chadwell said. "I am."

"Then you don't owe me any apologies, Billy, no matter how it turns out."

Chadwell grinned. "Mighty glad to hear you say that, Evan."

"You said there were four possibilities," Evan reminded him. "What's the fourth one?"

"Ah, now, that's the really interesting one." Chadwell held up a fourth finger and then closed his hand into a fist. "What if somebody shot *both* Johnny and Matt on purpose and deliberately made it look like they shot each other?"

Evan frowned. "Why the hell would anybody do that?"

"I don't know. But I think it's worth checking out."

"What do you want me to do?"

"You know the places where Johnny spent his time—" Chadwell began.

"Not really, but I know what part of town he liked the best. I could ask around down there, maybe find out if anybody else was holding a grudge against him. I know he had a few gambling debts." Evan found himself getting interested in the idea. "I also think we should check at the Double Eagle to see if Matt's story holds up."

"That's a good way to start," Chadwell agreed. "You get to work on that tomorrow, and I'll draft an impassioned opening statement for the trial."

Evan grinned. "Can't wait to hear that."

When Chadwell saw the grin on Evan's face, he knew that his plan was working. The young attorney's mind was quick and active, and even though this case resulted from a personal tragedy, Evan was being drawn into it and getting caught up in the mental challenge of ferreting out the facts.

In other words, the healing process had already begun.

Chapter Eleven

Evan went back to the office with Billy Chadwell and started mapping out the plan he would follow in his investigation. They had been there an hour when they heard heavy footsteps on the stairs outside. The door burst open a second later.

Axel Maddock strode into the room, his face taut with fury, and said without any greeting, "You never acted much like a real Maddock, boy, but I never figured you for a goddamned traitor!"

Slowly, Evan put down the pen that he had been using to make notes. He stared at his uncle. Axel's lean, leathery face was red with anger, and his knobby hands were clenched into fists. Evan had a pretty good idea what had put him in this condition.

"What do you mean by that?" he snapped back.

"You're helpin' a Lindsay, ain't you? That makes you a traitor!" Axel shook his head. "Never thought I'd see the day when a Maddock would try to help the man who shot his brother!"

Billy Chadwell spoke up. "Now see here, Axel. Like I told you yesterday, everybody is entitled to a defense in court, even a Lindsay."

"Shut up and stay out of this, Billy," Axel barked without looking at Chadwell. "This is between Evan and me."

Chadwell started to rise angrily from his chair, but Evan stopped him with a gesture. "I'll handle it, Billy," he said. He came to his feet and leaned over the table, matching his uncle glare for glare. "What Billy says is right, Uncle Axel. Everyone *is* entitled to a defense, but there's something even more important at stake here."

"More important than Johnny being shot down like a dog?"

Axel's harsh words sent a stab of pain lancing into Evan, but he swallowed the bitterness he felt. "It's Johnny I'm thinking about. Axel, did you ever stop to ask yourself what if Matt *didn't* kill Johnny? If he didn't, then the real killer is out there somewhere laughing because he got away with it, because he put something over on the Maddocks. Do you want that, Axel? Do you?"

Axel frowned at his nephew for a long moment, his attitude unbending. Finally he said, "Matt Lindsay killed Johnny. Couldn't have been no other way."

"Why? Why couldn't it have happened some other way?" Evan felt the frustration of trying to get through to Axel's already made up mind. "You don't believe Matt's story just because he's a Lindsay!"

"Reason enough," Axel said stiffly. "Besides, nobody else had any reason to kill Johnny."

"Johnny had gambling debts, Axel. I know that for a fact. And that's why I'm working with Billy on this case, to get the facts. Maybe Matt is guilty. If he is, that's what my investigation will confirm, and he'll still hang."

Axel shook his head. "That's just words, boy. They don't change the fact that you're takin' the Lindsays' side agin' your own. You can just consider yourself not a Maddock anymore, 'cause I sure as hell don't want you in my family after this!"

Evan took a deep breath and forced down the anger that he felt. "If that's the way you want it," he said quietly.

"That's the way I want it. You ain't welcome on my ranch anymore."

"All right," Evan agreed. "That's fine with me."

Axel raised one of his hands, shook the fist at Evan. "It was bad enough when that shyster partner of yours took Matt's case. You should've quit him as soon as you found out, boy! Instead you've thrown in with him and turned your back on your family! If I was twenty years younger, boy, I'd teach you a lesson you'd never forget."

Evan thought about the harsh words Axel had spoken and grinned tightly. "I wish you were, Axel," he said fervently. "I'd enjoy that right now. Now get the hell out of this office, old man. We've got work to do."

Axel looked shocked that Evan would say such things to him. He had been the leader of the family for so long that he expected blind obedience. It was obvious now that he was never going to get it from Evan Maddock.

"I'm goin'," he said. "But this ain't the end of this. Not by a long shot."

He stomped out, slamming the door behind him.

"I'm sorry, Billy," Evan said with a sigh. "The old goat had no right to say the things he did."

"Don't worry about that, Evan." Chadwell shook his head. "Maybe I made a mistake getting you involved with something that's liable to split you off from the rest of your family."

"It's been coming for a long time. I never have thought like the rest of the Maddocks." Evan rubbed the back of his neck, the weariness of this long, sad day taking its toll on him. "Their first reaction to any problem was always to reach for a gun. Maybe a clean break would be the best thing all around."

Unspoken was his real concern. He could live without Axel Maddock; that wouldn't be much of a hardship, since he and the old man had never been close. But he was starting to worry about how all this would affect Ted. This morning, when they had parted, Ted had made it clear that he didn't have much use now for his only remaining brother.

Whoever had pumped the bullet into Johnny might have killed even more than he thought.

Warren Prescott came into the Trainor hotel suite with a smile on his face and a piece of paper in his hand. "It's here, sir," he said, extending the paper to Trainor.

The senator took the telegraph blank and unfolded it. He knew what it was even before he read the words, but still it was good to see them in cold type. "It's official," he announced to Kathy and Prescott. "The attorney general has appointed me as the special prosecutor for Matt Lindsay's murder trial."

"I have some more good news," Prescott said. "I've been down to the courthouse, and the circuit judge will arrive in two days. The trial can start the day after he arrives."

It had been decided in the meetings between Trainor and District Attorney Hadley that the case would be tried before the circuit judge rather than the local county judge, who, like Hadley, knew both families involved quite well. They were going to do everything possible to ensure a fair, impartial trial.

That decision had rested well with Prescott, too, since he knew that the circuit judge in this area, the Honorable Leander Gardner, had a reputation for being tough on lawbreakers.

There was no doubt in Prescott's mind that Matt Lindsay would hang. The public would see him as a vicious killer brought to justice by the efforts of Howell Trainor.

And Prescott and Trainor would ride that hanging corpse right into the governor's mansion.

Trainor raised his eyebrows at Prescott's announcement that the trial was only three days off. "Western justice certainly moves quickly, doesn't it?" he commented.

"A speedy trial makes a good impact in the press," Prescott said. "But there will still be time for the journalists to get here to cover the proceedings. I expect some of them to start showing up on tomorrow morning's train." Prescott rubbed his jaw in thought. "It's a shame that Lindsay and Maddock didn't argue over a woman in addition to this feud thing. That would have made an even better story."

Trainor nodded in agreement. "More newspapers might have sent correspondents if that had been the case. Nevertheless, we must proceed with what we have, I suppose. It should still be enough to guarantee that everyone who goes to the polls will know that the name of Howell Trainor stands for law and order."

Kathy was sitting in an armchair close to the window, but now she stood up and said heatedly, "Doesn't this mean anything more to you than some sort of political advantage? One man is already dead and another is about to go to trial for his life, and all you can talk about is how much publicity you'll get for the campaign!"

Trainor frowned at his daughter in confusion. "But Matt Lindsay's a killer!" he said. "Why are you worried about him?"

"Are you sure he's a killer?" Kathy asked.

Trainor spread his hands. "The evidence seems clear enough to me. A bit circumstantial, perhaps, but surely enough to convince a jury beyond a shadow of a doubt that Lindsay killed young Maddock."

Kathy shook her head stubbornly but said nothing.

"Surely you don't believe his story," Trainor went on. He didn't enjoy arguing with his daughter and didn't understand why she suddenly seemed upset with him. "Or lack of story, I should say. Why, he hasn't even attempted to defend himself!"

"Exactly. If he was guilty, wouldn't he have tried to come up with some sort of story to explain things, to clear himself?" Kathy was following the same line of reasoning that had led Billy Chadwell to conclude that Matt might be innocent, though she wasn't aware of that coincidence.

Trainor stared at her, surprised that she was able to come up with such a complicated theory. Prescott was also surprised, and he didn't like Kathy's speculations. He didn't want her to do anything that might get in the way of his plans.

"I'm sorry, Kathy," he said. "I just can't put any credence in that idea. You're giving Matt Lindsay credit for more intelligence than he really has. He didn't come up with a story because he couldn't think quickly enough to invent a plausible one."

"And besides, if he's innocent, that ruins your story for the press, doesn't it?" she snapped.

"Kathy!" Trainor exclaimed, hurt by the sarcastic tone of her voice.

She shook her head, clearly angry, and went to her bedroom, shutting the door firmly behind her.

Trainor stared at the closed door, wondering why his daughter had turned on him. Prescott said gently, "Don't worry about her, sir. She'll come around once the trial starts."

"I hope so," Trainor said.

Prescott hoped so, too. The last thing he needed was for Trainor to get distracted and lose the case through sheer incompetence.

"Hold that board tight, now!" Nacho Newcomb told Ted as he poised the hammer over the plank they were nailing into place in the fence surrounding the big main corral.

Nacho had managed to keep Ted busy most of the afternoon as the two of them did the odd jobs that always needed doing around a ranch. For the time being, Nacho was content to leave the actual running of the spread to the hands. They were a good crew; they wouldn't let him down. It was more important right now that he keep an eye on Ted.

The boy was still sullen, though he hadn't resisted when Nacho suggested that they catch up on the chores. He had worn the Colt in the holster strapped around his waist until they got to this repair job on the corral. Then he had taken it off and draped the holster and shell belt over the top rail, where it was still handy.

Nacho kept up a running chatter all through the long afternoon, talking of anything and everything except Johnny's death and its aftermath. But he knew he wasn't getting through to Ted. The set of the boy's jaw told him that much.

The sound of horses made both of them look up from their work. Axel Maddock was riding into the ranch yard, several of his men following close behind him.

Axel reined in his horse and looked down at them, his

face set in its perennial glower. "I've got something to say to you, Ted," he snapped.

Ted just looked up at him and waited.

"Your brother's gone over to the other side, boy," Axel went on. "He might as well be a Lindsay. How about coming to live with me?"

Nacho's heart sank. He knew that Evan didn't want Ted knowing just yet of his involvement with Matt's defense, but now Axel had spoiled that.

"What are you talking about, Uncle Axel?" Ted asked.

Nacho stepped forward, hoping to forestall having it put into words, but Axel's riders suddenly put their hands on their gun butts.

Axel glared at Nacho and then leaned forward in the saddle and said, "Evan is helping Billy Chadwell to defend Matt Lindsay. He's stickin' up for the man who killed your brother!"

Ted's face paled. "No! That's a lie!" He turned to Nacho. "That's a lie, isn't it, Nacho?"

Nacho shrugged his broad shoulders helplessly, and Ted read the truth on his bearded face.

Ted couldn't believe it, yet Nacho wasn't denying what Axel said. Evan wasn't even here to deny it himself. Ted had been drawing on his anger at Johnny's death to keep him going, but now this new blow slammed into him and devastated all his defenses. He had grown up knowing that Evan and Johnny were all he had to hold onto. Now, in the space of a few days, they had both been taken from him, Johnny by death and Evan by his betrayal of his own family.

Ted reached out for his gun and holster. "You bet I'll go with you," he said, his voice as cold as a blue norther.

Axel nodded savagely. "Good. Go get your gear and saddle your horse. We'll wait right here for you."

Nacho said desperately, "You can't do this, Ted. When Evan finds out—"

Ted was already stalking away toward the house. "You tell Evan to go to hell," he flung back over his shoulder.

Nacho looked up at Axel, his face tight with anger, as he calculated his chances of running them off the ranch, of stopping Ted. He was outnumbered and outgunned, and there were no other hands nearby to come to his assistance.

"I know what you're thinkin', Newcomb," Axel snapped, "and I'm warnin' you. You may be a real bruiser, but you ain't got a chance here. The boy wants to go with me, and he's goin'."

Nacho spat in the dust. "We will see what Evan has to say about this."

"Evan Maddock don't scare me," Axel replied arrogantly.

Less than ten minutes later, Ted rode away from the ranch house beside Axel as Nacho stared bleakly after them. The big man shook his head.

It was beginning to seem as if the trouble would never end for the Maddock family.

Chapter Twelve

The sun had already dipped down behind the mountains, and stars were starting to twinkle in the deep blue sky overhead when Evan rode into the yard of the ranch house and swung down from the saddle.

He was tired. He had spent the rest of the afternoon going from bar to cantina to brothel in Pecos's red-light district. That was where Johnny had spent most of his time away from the ranch, and Evan had hoped that he could find someone who might tell him something useful. He had remembered that Johnny was trying to borrow money the day before his death. Though Johnny had denied it, Evan was sure that money was intended to cover a gambling debt.

Maybe Johnny hadn't been able to come up with the two hundred dollars in time. Maybe the man he owed it to had gotten tired of waiting and decided to make an example of him.

Evan's efforts had been fruitless so far, though. Business was slow in the places he visited; life didn't really get under way in that part of town until the sun went down. The bartenders and saloon girls he talked to seemed grateful for the break in their dull lives, but they told him nothing that led him any closer to another suspect in the killing.

He wasn't sure if his lack of success was due to the natural reluctance of those people to tell everything they knew to someone connected with the law—or if there just wasn't anything to find. Maybe Matt really was guilty. To his surprise, Evan had found himself starting to doubt that. When he was telling off old Axel, he more than half

149

believed what he was saying about the possibility of another killer.

He would have to hurry if he was going to uncover anything in time, though. He had heard from Chadwell, when he returned to the office in the late afternoon, that Judge Leander Gardner would arrive in a couple of days and that the trial would start the day after that.

Time was going to be running out before he knew it.

He supposed he should be back in Pecos tonight, making more rounds of Johnny's usual haunts, but he was worried about Ted. Solving Johnny's murder was important, but Ted was still alive and still needed him.

Moving with the slow gait of a man who is drained both physically and emotionally, Evan started up onto the veranda. The door of the house opened, and Nacho stepped out into the early evening shadows.

"Bad news, Evan," he said softly.

Evan stopped where he was, one foot on the steps, one foot still on the ground. "What is it?" he asked.

"Ted left. He went to stay with Axel."

The words hit Evan like a hammer blow between the eyes. The loss was complete now, the utter destruction of his family finished. He stared up at Nacho for a moment and then wheeled and went back to his horse.

"Where are you going?" Nacho called after him.

Evan pulled himself into the saddle and reined the animal around. "To get my brother back," he said flatly.

Then he put the spurs to the horse and galloped away from the house.

"Dammit!" Nacho reached back into the house, grabbed his sombrero from the peg just inside the door, and hurried down the steps. Two minutes later, he was racing after Evan on his own horse. The state Evan was in, it wasn't safe to let him go over to Axel's place by himself.

Evan pushed his horse hard. He knew the trail between the two ranches like the back of his own hand, and he didn't slow down when full dark fell before he had gone a mile. He faintly heard hoofbeats behind him, looked back over his shoulder, and recognized Nacho in the moonlight.

By the time they reached Axel Maddock's house, Nacho had cut the gap slightly because his horse had been rested, while Evan's was tired from the ride out from Pecos. Nacho was still a couple of hundred yards behind when Evan leaped down from the saddle and strode swiftly toward the house.

Two punchers appeared on the porch. They must have been expecting him, because one of them said, "You ain't welcome here, Evan. The boss says to throw you off his place."

Evan didn't slow down. He started up the steps and said, "My quarrel's not with you, Hank."

"Maybe it is," the cowboy said roughly. "I liked Johnny."

He launched a fist at Evan's head.

Evan ducked under the blow and came up with one of his own, driving his fist deep into the man's belly. The man gasped and doubled over. Evan hooked a left to his jaw and knocked him sprawling in the dust.

He sensed motion just above him and looked up to see that the other puncher had pulled his revolver. He slashed at Evan's head with the weapon.

A Winchester cracked in the night, and the man jerked his revolver back as splinters flew from the porch post a few inches from his face. Nacho's horse pounded into the yard as the big vaquero levered another shell into the chamber of the rifle. "Next one won't miss!" he yelled as he jerked the horse to a stop.

The door of the house banged open, and Axel Maddock stood there, his own Winchester in his hands. Ted stepped through the doorway behind him.

In the glow from the lamps in the house, Evan could see that Ted's face was set in hard lines. He felt his heart sink at what he saw there. Still, he had to try. "I've come to take you home, Ted," he said.

"This is my home now," Ted replied curtly.

Evan looked at his uncle. "Axel, you've got to talk to the boy."

"Already done my talkin'," Axel growled. "Told the boy how you was betrayin' your own family. Ted agrees

with me. Neither one of us wants anything more to do
with you, Evan. If I was you, I'd leave a place where I
wasn't welcome."

Evan looked past Axel to Ted. "I don't know what he
told you, Ted, but I'm not doing anything wrong."

"Are you defending Matt Lindsay for shooting Johnny?"

"Not exactly defending him, but I'm doing some investigative work in order to find out—"

"That's enough. So long, Evan." Ted turned and went
back into the house.

Evan looked long and hard at Axel and then said,
"Damn you."

"Boy made his own choice, just like you did," Axel
told him. "Now get off my land."

A new voice spoke from the shadows of the porch.
"Let the boy go home, Axel."

Axel's head jerked around. "Reba! What are you doin'
out here, woman?"

Reba Maddock emerged from the gloom, her face
twisted with emotion. "Please, Axel, let Ted go. I . . . I
never spoke up against you before, but don't do this to
him."

Axel harrumphed. "Ted made up his own mind—" he
began.

"After you poisoned it, after you turned him against
his own brother!" Anguish made Reba's voice crack. "Just
like you poisoned the minds of our own boys! Axel, I'm
tired of buryin' sons and nephews! God . . ." She raised
her apron and covered her face with it as tears started to
flow down her cheeks. "God, I'm so tired of buryin'. . . ."

Axel drew a long breath and blew it out through his
nose, clearly unsure what to do in the face of this unex-
pected opposition. After a moment, he repeated, "The
boy made up his own mind."

Reba turned and disappeared around the corner of
the porch, but her sobs were audible until another door
slammed.

Axel glanced back at Evan. "You still here?"

"I'm going," Evan said. There was nothing he could
do here short of fighting Axel and all of his men and trying

to drag Ted back home forcibly. He wasn't sure he could do that, even with the formidable Nacho to back him up, and he knew that he didn't want to.

Much as Evan hated to admit it, Axel was right. Ted had made his own choice. And for the moment, there was not one damn thing Evan could do about it.

He went to his horse and mounted. "Let's go, Nacho," he said softly as he turned the horse's head toward home.

Nacho backed his own horse out of the yard, keeping an eye on Axel Maddock and the two punchers. The one Evan had knocked down had hauled himself to his feet by now, and both men looked as if they'd continue the fight given half a chance.

Nacho didn't give them even that much. They knew what kind of shot he was with a rifle, knew that in the mood he was in he wouldn't hesitate to drop either one of them. When he was out of the yard, Nacho wheeled the horse and raced after Evan.

He came up even with him a few hundred yards later. Evan glanced over at the foreman and said, "You head on back to the ranch, Nacho."

"What are you going to do?"

"There's nothing out here for me. I'm going back to Pecos."

"I'm not sure that's a good idea, Evan—"

"Just do what I say, all right?" The hard tone of Evan's voice made it clear that arguing would do no good.

He turned his horse toward the north and took off across country. He didn't need a trail to find his way, not around here.

As Nacho watched him disappear into the night, he shook his head in dismay. This was going to be a long night for Evan Maddock.

Evan stared down into the glass of tequila and asked himself what he was doing here in this cantina. The answer was simple, he thought fuzzily: He was getting good and drunk.

He had wandered through the streets of Pecos for a time after stabling his horse, and when he found himself in the same part of town where he had been asking questions that afternoon, he had decided to stop in for a drink.

One drink had become several, and he didn't feel like stopping. By now he was well on his way to being drunk.

Just like Johnny had been that night.

The thought made him shove the glass away. Sure, he could drink until all the problems were blotted out, but they would come right back when he sobered up. All he'd really get out of it was one hell of a headache in the morning.

He put his hands on the table and shoved himself up. Leaving a coin on the table to cover what he had drunk, he made his way to the door of the cantina and went out into the night. He hated to leave the dark, smoky atmosphere of the place; the squalor of it matched his mood.

Maybe if he went back to the office and did some paperwork, something he'd really have to concentrate on, that would help clear the cobwebs from his brain. From here on out, he intended to throw himself into his work. After all, it was all he had left.

He turned down an alley, knowing it to be a shortcut back to the main part of town. He had only gone a few feet when some instinct warned him, and he glanced back over his shoulder.

He saw only a fast-moving shadow, a deeper patch of darkness in the night. Evan threw himself to the side. A stray beam of illumination flickered off something shiny, and he felt a ripping in his coat, a sudden fire in his arm.

Nothing like cold steel to sober a man up.

Evan stepped in close to his attacker and rammed a shoulder against him. Both men staggered, and Evan threw a hand up. His fingers brushed against a wrist, and he grabbed it and held on for dear life. The other man tried to knee him, but he turned and took the blow on his thigh.

Evan lashed out with his free hand and felt it slam into flesh. The attacker grunted in pain, and Evan twisted his wrist savagely. The knife fell to the dirt floor of the alley with a soft thud. Evan shoved the man away and stopped, his hand sliding over the dirt until he touched the handle of the knife.

He slashed the blade in front of him as his opponent charged again. The man gasped and lurched away. Evan heard the rapid staccato of his running footsteps as he raced away down the alley. For a moment, red rage blinding him, he started to give chase. The urge to hurt, to strike out, filled him. But he caught himself and stopped there in the alley, drawing deep draughts of air into his lungs.

He had been lucky this time. If he pushed the fight, he might wind up dead. He still had too many things to do to let that happen.

Dropping the knife in the alley, he turned back toward his office. His arm was starting to throb, and he could feel a sticky wetness on his sleeve.

The arm was really hurting by the time he reached the office and got a lamp lit. He peeled off his coat and shirt and found an ugly gash in his upper left arm. If he hadn't moved aside when he did, the knife thrust would have gone home to his heart.

He was binding up the wound as best he could when the office door opened and Billy Chadwell stepped in. Chadwell said, "Saw the light on when I was going by downstairs. Working late, Ev—?" He saw what Evan was doing and grunted in surprise. "My God, what happened to you?"

"Somebody didn't take a liking to me," Evan said dryly. He explained what had happened as Chadwell helped him bandage the wound.

When they were done, Chadwell stepped back and said, "This proves Matt is innocent, Evan. The real killer knew you were asking questions and tried to stop you. That proves we're onto something."

"It proves I'm a damn fool for walking through that part of town when I'd had too much to drink," Evan said. "People get knifed and robbed down there all the time, Billy. You know that."

Chadwell wagged a finger at him. "In the legal world, there are no such things as coincidences. There's a cause and effect for everything. I tell you we're on the right trail."

"Maybe so, but I'm not going to do any more trailing tonight. This arm's starting to stiffen up."

"You'd best have Doc look at it first thing in the morning—even better, right away."

Evan shook his head. "Tomorrow's soon enough. Right now all I want is to get some sleep."

Chadwell went down the stairs behind him. "Walk careful, Evan," he cautioned. "We've got somebody worried enough to kill. Again."

Evan nodded. He didn't put much stock in Chadwell's theory, but as he walked back to the rooming house, he kept an eye out behind him just in case.

And when he got to his room, he took his old Colt out of a drawer, thumbed cartridges into the cylinder, and slipped it under his pillow.

There was no point, after all, in taking unnecessary chances.

Warren Prescott opened the door of his hotel room and saw a pale, sweating Cal Ahern standing there out of breath. There was a red stain on Ahern's frilly white shirt. Before Ahern could say anything, Prescott snapped, "The alley behind the hotel in ten minutes. I'll be there." And then he shut the door in Ahern's face.

Prescott closed his eyes and took several deep breaths. When he had answered the knock on his door, he hadn't expected to find Ahern there again. It was obvious that the gambler had once again done something stupid. This situation couldn't go on.

Prescott slipped into his coat and hat and left the hotel through the rear door. No one saw him leave, which was the way he wanted it. He was sick and tired of taking unnecessary chances.

Ahern was waiting in the alley as Prescott had instructed. Prescott came up to him and snapped, "All right, what happened?"

"Maddock's onto me!" Ahern exclaimed rapidly. "He's

been hanging around all day asking questions about his brother, and tonight he was back in the cantina!"

"What was he doing?"

"Just drinking. But I know he was really after me!"

Prescott sighed. Ahern was weak, and he was scared. Not a good combination. "What did you do?" he asked.

"I followed him. He went down an alley, and I tried to finish him off with a knife." Ahern almost sobbed. "The bastard took it away from me. He cut me!"

"You damned fool!" Prescott hissed, unable to control his anger. "You might as well have told them that Lindsay is innocent. Maddock and Chadwell aren't fools. They'll figure out why you made such a stupid move."

"I don't care what you say about me anymore," Ahern returned sullenly. "I'm getting out of Pecos. Tonight."

"Perhaps that wouldn't be such a bad idea. Where will you go?"

"Flores has a place he can hide me out for a couple of days," Ahern said. "Then I'll head for the border. He has friends in Mexico. . . . Once I get across the line, nobody will ever be able to track me."

"Flores? The cantina owner?"

Ahern snorted. "That cantina makes him some money, all right, but it's really just a front. He's got a finger in every dirty game in this part of the country."

Prescott rubbed his jaw. "A man who can be bought, eh?" he said speculatively.

"Damn right. But to do it, I'll need more money." Ahern was almost whining by this point.

Prescott reached under his coat. "I was afraid it would come to this. How much do you want?"

Greed crept into Ahern's voice as he said, "A thousand would do nice."

"Fine," Prescott snapped. He withdrew his hand from under his coat.

Then he jammed the two-shot derringer he was holding into Ahern's belly and triggered both barrels.

The shots were muffled by Ahern's body. The gambler staggered and opened his mouth to cry out as he felt the slugs tear through his midsection, but Prescott's free hand clapped over Ahern's mouth in a cruel grip. Both men sprawled in the dirt of the alley. Ahern tried to throw Prescott's weight off him, but his strength was running out along with his blood.

Prescott held him down until he was limp and unmoving.

As he stood up and bent to grasp Ahern's body, Prescott cursed in a low, vehement voice. He had to get rid of the carcass now. He was sure that the shots couldn't have been heard more than a few feet away, but he couldn't leave Ahern here to be discovered. If Ahern was found, there was a chance that his death would be passed off as unrelated to Johnny Maddock's murder, but Prescott didn't want to take that chance. Yet he didn't have a horse to cart Ahern's body away—and he didn't want to risk being caught stealing one. Still, he wanted his trail covered. For that, he would need help.

He thought he had a pretty good idea where to turn.

Gunther Wagner lifted his head from the pillow of the bunk in his small room. He thought he had heard something. Beside him, Mary Killane stirred, her head nestled against his shoulder.

This rendezvous had been her idea, but Gunther hadn't objected too much. To his extreme pleasure, he had found out that he had been right about the passionate nature lurking under Mary's reserved exterior. Now she would probably expect him to marry her.

And for some strange reason, that idea didn't bother Gunther at all.

At the moment, though, he was puzzled by the sounds of someone moving around outside. He was charged with guarding the special stagecoach, so he had to find out who was skulking around in the night. He didn't know why anyone would want to steal an empty coach, but you never could tell what people would do.

He slipped out of bed. Mary murmured something in a drowsy voice, and Gunther whispered, "I'll be right back, sweetheart." She snuggled deeper into the pillow and went back to sleep.

Gunther stepped into his pants and cat-footed his way through the stable. The door was open a few inches, and he stood there silently as he heard stealthy footsteps coming along the alley. He knew he couldn't be seen from outside.

Then he relaxed and grinned as he saw Warren Prescott hurry past the stable. Looked like Prescott was up to his old tricks, Gunther thought. But it was no business of his if Prescott slipped off to a saloon or a whorehouse. Hell, working for Howell Trainor would make anybody go looking for some pleasure.

Gunther grinned, shook his head, and went back to the little bunkroom. Back to Mary . . .

Chapter Thirteen

Evan wasn't sure what made him go into the dining room of the hotel where the Trainors were staying for his breakfast the next morning. There were several cafés where he could have eaten. But after paying an early morning visit to the doctor, who bandaged the wound properly, Evan found himself strolling into the hotel.

Kathy Trainor was just sitting down to breakfast in the hotel dining room when she looked up and saw Evan standing in the archway leading to the hotel lobby. His arm was bandaged, and he looked pale. She called his name, and he looked over at her and smiled and then made his way across the room to her table.

"Morning, Miss Trainor," he said, holding his hat in his hands. "How are you?"

"I'm fine," she said. "But how are *you*, Mr. Maddock? That seems more to the point." She glanced at his arm.

"Oh, I'm all right, I suppose." He fell silent.

She decided not to question him further. If he wanted her to know how he had gotten his injury, he would tell her.

At least, she thought, he looked better than the last time she had seen him. Though Johnny's death was still very recent and vivid, some of the immediate shock had worn off. Evan seemed to be coping with his grief.

Kathy indicated the chair across the table. "Won't you join me?"

Evan looked a bit surprised, but he nodded and said, "Of course," and sat down.

Kathy wasn't sure why she had invited him to sit with her, but she didn't regret the invitation. She saw Evan

Maddock in a different light now. She knew now that he had no part in the feud, that he despised such behavior because it had led to the death of his brother. She regretted some of the things she had said to him, the harsh accusations and the angry words.

She would make it up to him now by being his friend, she decided. That wouldn't be difficult; he was a handsome, intelligent man, the kind of man that some of her flighty friends in Austin would be all a-twitter over.

She told herself that was not the case with her, however. She had no romantic interest in Evan—did she?

"Appreciate you asking me to join you," Evan said, breaking into her train of thought. "I usually have breakfast with Billy, but he doesn't seem to be around this morning. Anyway, you're a whole lot prettier."

The compliment startled her, but she recovered quickly. "Thank you," she said, and there was no hint of embarrassment in her manner.

A waiter came and took their orders, and while they were waiting for their food, Kathy asked, "Have you made any progress on your case? Unless you don't want to talk about it, of course. I'll understand if you don't."

Evan shook his head. "I don't mind talking about it. Johnny's gone, and nothing can change that, but I still have to work for justice, no matter what the circumstances."

"My father and I were both surprised when we heard that you were helping Billy Chadwell with the case."

A wry smile touched Evan's lips. "My part in it was supposed to be behind the scenes. I guess it's hard to keep anything quiet in a city this size."

"You didn't answer my question," she gently reminded.

"Have we made any progress? Well, I'm not sure it would be appropriate to answer that question."

"Why? Because my father is the special prosecutor?"

"Seems like a good enough reason," Evan drawled.

Kathy shook her head firmly. "You're wrong about me. I'm not trying to pry for my father's sake. I happen to think there's a good chance Matt Lindsay may be innocent."

"Why do you say that?"

"It's . . . too pat," she said, searching for the words. "It looks too much like . . . what do you call it, a frame-up."

"That's what it's starting to look like to me, too," Evan agreed, his mouth going grim. "I've learned over the years to trust Billy's hunches, and he's got a hunch about this case." Evan's eyes met Kathy's gaze across the table. "I must admit, though, that you've surprised me. I thought you'd take your father's side."

Kathy hesitated and then said, "I love my father very much, but I've seen him use people before. He takes advantage of situations to further his political career. I'm probably being a disloyal daughter to say this, but he sees things in terms of how they'll affect him, rather than how people might be hurt."

"That's a politician, all right," Evan said.

His words struck a raw nerve. She'd heard this kind of denigration of politicians all too often in the past. A fire lit her eyes as she said, "You've never held office. You've got no right to paint all politicians with the same brush. Some of them genuinely try to help people."

Evan stubbornly shook his head. "None that I ever saw."

"Then maybe you should try to change the system from within. Why don't you run for office yourself sometime?"

"Not me," Evan said firmly. "I've got a law practice to worry about, and that's enough."

At that point, the waiter brought their plates from the kitchen, and both Evan and Kathy were grateful for the interruption. They had been getting along well until the brief clash over politics, and they wanted to keep it that way.

"How did you become a lawyer?" Kathy asked when the waiter was gone.

Evan was tackling a pile of flapjacks. He swallowed and said, "Billy sort of took me under his wing after my dad and two of my other brothers were killed. My mother died not long after. I guess it was natural that I'd drift into the same line of work as Billy; he was like a father to me during those first years after my parents died. And we never were able to prove who killed my dad and my brothers. I guess I saw the law as a way of resolving things without having to resort to killing."

"That's a refreshing attitude for this part of the country."

Evan shrugged. "Don't misunderstand me. There are times when you might have to fight for what's yours. But I always thought this feud was senseless."

"What started it, anyway? I don't think I've ever heard anyone mention the reason behind it."

A ironic smile tugged at Evan's mouth. "Could be that's because nobody really remembers. Axel and Jubal got into some sort of fuss about water rights, and then it really heated up when they both set their sights on the same woman."

"Did she marry one of them?"

"They were both already married, and the woman was a Mexican lady who wasn't really a lady, if you know what I mean."

Kathy colored in embarrassment. "Yes. I believe I do know what you mean. It's amazing how often a woman figures in a disagreement between two men."

"Some men go plumb loco over a woman, all right," Evan said. "Reckon I can understand it sometimes, too." He was looking intently at Kathy as he spoke, more intently than he realized.

His meaning wasn't lost on her, and she blushed even more.

Suddenly, Evan seemed to realize he had been staring at her, and he dug into his food with more vigor, as if eager to finish the meal and be on his way.

Their talk was meaningless chitchat from that point on, and when Evan was finished, he stood up and said, "I'd best be getting back to work. I enjoyed talking with you, Miss Trainor."

"I enjoyed it, too. But please, you must call me Kathy."

He nodded slowly. "All right, Kathy. And I'm Evan."

"Of course."

He smiled at her, shifted his hat awkwardly from hand to hand for a moment, and then turned and left the dining room. She saw him stop to pay the clerk at the desk for his meal, and then he hurried out of the hotel.

Kathy took a deep breath. Unless she was badly mistaken, she had learned one thing this morning—Evan Maddock was smitten with her.

In a few days, though, after the trial, she would be leaving Pecos and would most likely never see him again. That would probably be the best thing all around—because she was afraid that she might be falling in love with him, too.

In an armchair in the lobby, Warren Prescott lowered the newspaper he had been pretending to read and studied Kathy's face. He knew that look; he had seen it on the faces of other women. She was in love with Evan Maddock, in love with the goddamned small-town lawyer! He had seen them sitting together when he came into the lobby and had dropped into this chair to watch them surreptitiously. The situation was clear to him now. His pulse pounded angrily in his veins as he thought about what had happened right under his nose.

It was a shame Ahern had missed with that knife.

When the trial was over, though, Prescott would see about making other arrangements for taking care of Mr. Evan Maddock. He would never have Kathy—Prescott would see to that.

Before the year was out, he vowed, Kathy would be Mrs. Warren Prescott, no matter what he had to do.

That day and the next passed quickly, too quickly for Evan. Judge Gardner arrived in Pecos, met briefly with Chadwell and Trainor, and set jury selection to begin at nine o'clock the next morning.

So far, Evan had turned up absolutely nothing to indicate that someone else might have killed Johnny. He had checked Matt's story about the Double Eagle and had learned nothing to cause him to doubt it. He had spent hours questioning the denizens of Pecos's red-light district, asking the same questions again and again and getting the same frustrating answers.

The next evening, following jury selection, Matt Lindsay must have read the truth on Evan's face as Evan came into the cellblock. Darkness had fallen, and in a little over twelve hours, Matt would go into the courtroom and put his life on the line.

"No luck, huh?" Matt said as he leaned on the bars of his cell. Most of his normal color had returned, and he was healing well from the gunshot wound.

Evan shook his head. "No luck," he agreed. He pulled the three-legged stool over in front of the cell and sat down wearily.

Matt turned away from the bars and paced over to the high window, moving like a caged animal. Without looking at Evan, he asked, "Now that the jury's been selected, how long do you think the trial will last?"

"Considering the amount of evidence each side has to present . . . not more than another day, I'm afraid."

"Then by this time tomorrow night, I'll be hangin' from the gallows." Matt's voice shook slightly, despite his efforts to keep it steady.

"I haven't given up yet," Evan said stubbornly. No matter how bad the situation looked, he didn't want Matt to give up hope. Maybe he was a traitor to his own family, but he had found himself growing to like Matt over the last couple of days. The experience of being shot and then thrown in jail and charged with murder had changed the young man. The arrogance had drained away from him, and he wasn't the hotheaded troublemaker that he had once been.

Now Matt said resignedly, "It's my own fault, I reckon. Wish I'd never tried to goad Johnny into drawin'. He really wasn't a bad sort, for a Maddock. No offense, Evan."

Evan smiled and waved off the comment. Old habits died hard.

Matt went on, "I just saw red when I came in and Johnny was tryin' to lord it over that gambler. He got such a kick out of puttin' a scare into him."

Evan's head snapped up. "What gambler?"

"I never caught his name. Just a fella who hung

around down at the Flores Cantina a lot. Think he had something goin' with one of Flores's gals."

"I don't remember you mentioning this gambler before," Evan said with a frown.

Matt turned to face him and shrugged. "I just remembered that part of it. Bein' shot does funny things to your brain, Evan."

"Nobody else mentioned it, either."

"Folks down in that part of town don't talk much to outsiders. They don't want to get anybody else into trouble, so it's hard to get a straight answer out of 'em."

"I noticed that," Evan said. His mind was racing. This could be the break he had been looking for. If he could only locate this gambler. . . . "What did the gambler look like?"

"Curly hair, sort of sandy-colored, lean in the face. And he dressed pretty well. 'Course, you expect that from a gambler."

Evan put his hands on his knees and stood up from the stool. He was mentally cursing himself for not turning up this lead earlier, but he kept his face and voice noncommittal as he said, "Think I'll go poke around some more, Matt. Keep your chin up."

"Sure," Matt said mockingly. "The noose fits better over the head that way."

Evan returned the bleak grin that Matt gave him, and then he left the cellblock. Sheriff Ring looked up from his desk as Evan went through the outer office and asked, "You ready for the trial tomorrow, Maddock?"

"I will be," Evan declared.

As he walked rapidly toward the Flores Cantina, he went back over the pieces of the puzzle. He was certain that the money Johnny had tried to borrow was intended to pay off a debt to the gambler that Matt had mentioned. Lacking the money, Johnny had publicly bullied the gambler into waiting. That could create quite a grudge.

But one that would lead to murder? Evan intended to find out.

The cantina didn't seem too busy tonight, he thought as he pushed through the swinging doors into its smoky interior. All of Pecos was quieter than normal, which meant that a lot of people were making an early evening of it. The trial would start bright and early, and most of the population would be on hand to watch Matt's fate being decided.

Evan cast his eyes around the room, but he didn't see anyone matching the description that Matt had given him of the gambler. A few cowboys were drinking and playing cards, and most of the bar girls were sitting around looking bored, their services in no great demand tonight. Tomorrow night, after the hanging—if there was one—the place would be booming with trade. There was nothing like seeing someone else die to make people want to live it up.

Evan went to the bar and nodded to Flores. The fat little man asked, "You want something to drink, Señor Maddock?"

Evan shook his head. "Not tonight. I'm looking for somebody." He gave Flores the description of the man he was looking for.

Flores lifted his shoulders and spread his hands. "Sorry, Señor Maddock. I don't know the man."

Evan felt a surge of anger. He had been watching Flores's eyes, and he was sure he had seen a flicker of recognition as he described the gambler. Flores was lying to him.

Losing his temper wouldn't do any good, though. Evan swallowed his anger and said, "You're sure?"

"Sí, señor. I am sure."

One of the bar girls was lounging against the bar a few feet from where Evan stood, and now she straightened and sauntered toward him. She stepped up close beside him, but Evan barely gave her a glance, seeing only a Mexican whore with red-rimmed eyes.

"You want to go out back with me, señor?" she asked throatily. "I show you a very good time."

It was the most blatant proposition Evan had ever received, though it was no secret that the girls were selling their bodies in the shacks behind the place. He started to shake his head and send her on her way when she leaned seductively against him—and he felt the prick of a knife blade against his side.

He stiffened as she whispered softly, "I think you should go outside with me, señor."

Evan thought about trying to thrust her away before she could stab him, but there was a fierce light burning in her eyes, a light that said she would enjoy seeing his blood. This made no sense . . . which meant that it might have some connection with the case.

"All right," he said. "I'll go."

She leaned her head against his shoulder and slipped her arm around his waist as they walked toward the rear door of the cantina. Flores watched them go, a strange expression on his face.

When they reached the deep shadows of the alley between the cantina and the shacks, the woman abruptly sprang away from him. She held the knife in plain sight now, ready to dart forward and bury it in his flesh.

"You bastard!" she hissed. "What have you done with Cal?"

Evan took a deep breath. "Afraid I don't know what you're talking about, ma'am."

"Do not mock me! I hear you describe him to Flores. Where is he?"

"I don't know. That's why I was asking Flores. I don't even know the man's name."

"His name is Cal Ahern. I am Celestina."

"And you say Ahern is missing?"

"Not for two days now have I seen him." Her voice shook, but the hand that held the knife was rock steady. "I am so afraid. I fear that something has happened to him."

"Well, Celestina, my name is Evan Maddock. I'm a lawyer, and I just want to ask Ahern some questions."

"You do not know where he is?"

"I wish I did," Evan said sincerely.

"He said that when he left Pecos he would take me with him." Celestina was having a hard time fighting back the tears now, as two days of worrying caught up with her. The hand holding the knife dipped down, and Evan could have disarmed her, but he didn't think she was a threat to him anymore. "I knew he should not have talked to that man," she went on, almost wailing.

"What man?" Evan asked.

"The one in the fancy clothes. The one from Austin."

Evan's heart was suddenly slugging as hard as it had when he found Johnny's body. He knew then that Celestina might be the key to this whole case.

"Are you talking about Howell Trainor?" he asked, hardly daring to believe the wild theory that had just popped into his head.

"No, no, the other one. The young one, the man with the hard eyes."

"Prescott . . ." Evan whispered.

Like that it fell into place. He didn't know all the details yet or the exact reasons behind it, but he was sure that Warren Prescott, with the help of Cal Ahern, was responsible for Johnny's death. Prescott and Ahern had framed Matt Lindsay for the killing, and it looked like they were on the verge of getting away with it, unless he could come up with some proof.

The first thing was to take Celestina and go wake up Billy Chadwell. He could leave the woman with Billy and let him get her story while he tried to locate Ahern. It might take all night, but it was worth losing a little sleep.

"Celestina, will you come with me? I want you to talk to a friend of mine and tell him everything you saw going on with Ahern and this man from Austin. I promise you, we'll get to the bottom of this and find your friend."

It was hard to read her face in the gloom, but she stepped toward him and nodded. "Sí, I will help—" She broke off with a little cry.

Evan heard a scuttling sound behind him and tried to turn. He wasn't quite quick enough, and something slammed into the side of his head. The night seemed to explode into brilliant flashes of light, and then he was pitching forward into a darkness deeper than any he had ever known.

Ramirio Flores leaped across Evan's unconscious body and grabbed Celestina, wrenching the knife out of her hand. He swung up the shotgun he had used to knock

Evan out and cursed the woman in explosive Spanish. His tirade was cut short by a curt command from the shadows.

"That's enough, Flores," Warren Prescott said. "Maddock's figured out too much. You'll have to take care of him. I can't afford to have him at that trial."

"Sí." Flores shook the sobbing Celestina. "And what about the girl?"

Prescott sauntered out into the alley and stopped in front of Celestina. She was breathing deeply with fright. Prescott lifted his hand and caressed her cheek for a moment. He smiled regretfully. "She knows too much. I'm afraid she'll have to die, too."

Flores nodded as Celestina cringed away from Prescott. "I will tie them up and gag them. They will be safe in one of the shacks until morning—tonight I must stay at the cantina, so no one will notice anything different. Tomorrow I take them to a place I know, out on the edge of the desert. No one close by. It will be perfect."

"Fine, fine," Prescott said impatiently. "Tomorrow, then, while the trial is going on. Fitting, I suppose."

Celestina suddenly conquered her fear for a moment and spat at him in a gesture of defiance. The spittle struck Prescott's cheek. He recoiled and then savagely backhanded her across the face.

"I'd like to take care of you myself, you little bitch," he said. "You almost ruined everything. I'm trusting you to take care of this, Flores."

"Sí, you will not be disappointed. You will be glad you decided to hire me, señor. I take care of them just like I helped you with Ahern, sí?"

Prescott nodded curtly and then faded away in the shadows, leaving Flores there with Celestina and the unconscious Evan Maddock.

It had been a near thing, Prescott thought as he walked back toward the hotel. If Flores hadn't suspected something and sent a boy to fetch him . . . if Maddock had gotten Celestina into the hands of the law . . . if Ahern's body had been found . . .

But now there were no more ifs. Now it was over except for the trial. And Warren Prescott had *won*. . . .

Chapter Fourteen

The oldtimers were already saying it was going to be the hottest day of the year so far in Pecos. Even this early in the morning the heat was oppressive, and Billy Chadwell knew that the courtroom was going to be an oven.

He was seated at the defense table, a few papers spread out before him, more for appearance's sake than any other reason. Matt was being held by a couple of deputies in an anteroom. Across the narrow aisle at the prosecution table, Howell Trainor and Stephen Hadley were conferring in low voices. Warren Prescott was seated in the front row of the spectators' section, and from time to time he leaned over the low railing that divided the two areas and joined in the conversation.

The courtroom was beginning to fill up. Not everyone would be able to crowd into the rows of seats; some of the people would have to stand in the back of the room, and others would have to wait outside. This was the biggest thing to hit Pecos in a long time, and townsmen wanted to be able to say they had attended the trial of Matt Lindsay. Adding to the crush of people were the journalists sent to cover the trial; they were busy scribbling in their notepads.

The door of the anteroom opened, and the deputies led Matt out. He was handcuffed, and they brought him to the table before they removed the cuffs. He sat down next to Chadwell, rubbing his wrists where the metal had chafed the skin.

"Now I don't want you worrying about a thing, Matt," Chadwell said heartily. "This will be over with before you know it, and you'll be a free man."

The look in Matt's eyes told Chadwell that Matt knew he was lying.

The jury that had been selected the day before was ushered in next. A grim-looking bunch, Chadwell thought as they took their seats in the box. He felt a tap on his shoulder and turned to see Kathy Trainor leaning over the railing. "Why, hello, Miss Trainor," he said, surprised to find her there.

"Is Evan here?" Kathy asked. She was frowning in concern.

Her worry about Evan matched Chadwell's. "I haven't seen him since last night," he told her softly. "I don't know where he is, but I'm sure he'll be here." *He had better be, and with a miracle in his coat*, Chadwell thought grimly.

A commotion at the door made everyone turn around and look to see what was going on. The Maddock and Lindsay parties had arrived at the same time, and Axel and Jubal were standing in the doorway glaring at each other. Both of them were armed, as were their men, and Sheriff Ring was standing just inside the door arguing with them.

"I tell you, you can't come in here armed," Ring insisted loudly. "You'll get your guns back later, but for now you've got to give them up if you want to enter."

"I ain't sittin' in a room with a Lindsay unless I got a weapon," Axel barked.

"Well, I could say the same about them back-shootin' Maddocks," Jubal countered.

Sheriff Ring was adamant, though, and finally the two old men surrendered their Colts and motioned for their men to do likewise. Then both factions filed in and took seats on opposite sides of the courtroom, the Lindsays behind the defense table, the Maddocks behind the prosecution.

Billy Chadwell studied the hard faces of Axel and Jubal and would have been willing to bet that there was more than one gun concealed in their clothes. Hell, Ike Ring hadn't searched them; they could have an arsenal hidden away and be just waiting for the verdict before starting an all-out war.

Ted Maddock sat beside his uncle Axel, his face showing no emotion. The boy was still holding it in.

Howell Trainor felt the familiar butterflies in his stomach. Even after all these years, the anticipation got to him. He knew the tenseness would go away as soon as he started to speak. He glanced over at the defense table, and his eyes narrowed in surprise as he saw Kathy sitting directly behind it. He didn't know what had come over that young lady the last few days. She was certainly acting strangely.

Judge Leander Gardner came into the courtroom then, and everyone rose at the bailiff's command. Gardner was a white-haired old bulldog of a jurist, known and respected throughout the state. He gaveled the court to order, waited until everyone was seated again, and then rumbled, "Mr. Prosecutor, let's hear what you've got to say."

Trainor stood up, and immediately his nervousness was gone. With a firm, confident expression on his face, he launched into his opening statement.

Five miles west of Pecos, Evan Maddock was also worrying about the trial, but at the moment he had more pressing problems on his mind. His hands were tied behind his back, his feet lashed together, and he was sprawled on the dirt floor of a deserted cabin. Next to him was Celestina, who was tied the same way.

They could hear Ramirio Flores, outside the cabin, digging a grave big enough for two.

"Keep working at it," Evan urged Celestina. "The ropes feel a little looser now."

He had regained consciousness as Flores was bringing them out to the cabin in his wagon. Once Flores left them alone, Celestina had filled Evan in on what had happened in the alley the night before, and then he had told her to roll over next to him, back to back, so that she could try to untie the knots binding him. She had been working at the bonds for what seemed like hours, and her progress was too slow. Flores would be back any minute to finish them off.

Their time ran out even sooner than Evan had expected. He heard footsteps outside, and Flores stepped into the cabin, a shovel in one hand, a Winchester in the other. He grinned broadly when he saw their position on the floor.

"I tie the knots too good for you, no?" he gloated. "There will be no escape for you now."

"Please," Celestina pleaded. "Please do not kill us. I will do anything. . . . You can do what you wish to me. . . ."

"I already have, *puta*, many times. Or have you forgotten so soon?"

"Look, you don't have to do this," Evan said, a note of desperation edging into his voice. "We can work something out." He hated to grovel before this man, but he was stalling for time, for a chance, any kind of chance to strike back.

Flores laughed. "You got nothing I want, gringo. I'm already taking all I want from your family. Where do you think your uncle's cattle have been going, anyway?" He waved his hand to indicate the cabin. "My men, they bring the cattle here for the branding, then they take them on to the south. Eighty head are on their way right now. And old man Maddock, he always blames the Lindsays. A good plan, no?"

Evan said nothing, just stared stonily at Flores.

Flores dropped the shovel in the corner of the shack and took a knife from his belt. He wasn't grinning now. He stepped forward and slashed the ropes on their feet, moving back quickly so that Evan couldn't kick out at him. He jerked the barrel of the rifle in a commanding gesture. "On your feet, both of you."

With their hands tied behind their backs and their feet numb from the bindings, it took a few minutes for Evan and Celestina to clamber to their feet. Once they were standing, though, Flores ordered, "Outside."

They went out into the bright sunshine, Flores following behind them with the Winchester ready. Evan saw the gaping hole in the earth and knew what the cantina owner planned. He was going to march them up to the grave, shoot them in the back of the head, and let them topple into the hole.

"A nice grave, is it not?" Flores taunted them as they paused on the lip of the opening. "Nice and deep. The coyotes will not get you. This one is much better than the one I dug for Ahern after Señor Prescott killed him. *Aaiiee*, the coyotes will have him up in no time, and then they and the buzzards will have a feast, no?" He laughed raucously.

The laugh drove Celestina to madness. She spun around, screamed, and threw herself at him, no longer even aware of the threat of the rifle. Flores grunted in surprise and whipped the rifle around, smashing the butt against her head and knocking her to the side.

Evan, knowing that this was his last chance, was moving a split-second after Celestina. As she slumped to the ground from the blow, Evan launched himself at Flores. Before Flores could bring the rifle back to bear, Evan rammed into him with all his weight, knocking both of them to the hot, sandy ground.

Flores cried out as the Winchester slipped out of his fingers. He scrambled for the rifle, but before he could reach it Evan was on him, driving his knee up into Flores's groin. Flores screeched in pain.

Anger surged through Evan, driving him on and giving him a strength he didn't know he had. The awkwardness of being tied up barely slowed him down as he twisted away from Flores to get some room. He lashed out with his booted foot and felt a satisfying jar up his leg as the kick smashed Flores's nose, driving his head backward.

The Mexican went limp, and for a moment Evan was afraid he had killed him. But as he scrambled up on his knees and crawled over to Flores, he saw that the man was still breathing, though faintly. Evan turned around and reached behind him with his bound hands. His fingers touched the handle of Flores's knife and plucked it from his belt.

A few yards away, Celestina lay unmoving on the sand.

Evan sawed his own ropes loose, nicking himself a time or two but ignoring the minor wounds. Flores wasn't going to be waking up for a while, so he hurried over to Celestina and gently turned her onto her back.

There was a huge bruise on her head where Flores had clubbed her, and thin trails of blood leaked from her nose and ears. Evan knew she was hurt very badly. He cradled her head in his lap, and she opened her eyes and looked up at him.

She said something in Spanish, but Evan couldn't make out the words. Then she cried out, "Cal!" She stiffened in his arms.

A moment later, he closed her unseeing eyes.

He laid her down and stood up, bending to pick up the Winchester from where it had fallen. He felt like smashing Flores's skull with the butt, just as the Mexican had done to Celestina, but Evan controlled the murderous urge.

He had a better use for Ramirio Flores.

The prosecution had rested its case after calling only a few witnesses. Several of them testified that there was bad blood between Johnny and Matt and that it was Matt who tried to goad Johnny into a gunfight at the cantina—a fact that everyone in the courtroom knew. Warren Prescott had told the story of how the two bodies were discovered, and Howell Trainor used the opportunity to point out that the murder occurred on the trail to the Maddock ranch, nowhere near the Lindsay spread, which suggested that Matt had gone hunting for Johnny. Kathy Trainor wasn't called to corroborate Prescott's testimony; everyone knew that part of the story, too. Finally, the doctor had presented the medical evidence. The combined testimony suggested that Matt Lindsay was a cold-blooded killer who had followed Johnny out to his ranch and then ended his life.

Now it was up to Billy Chadwell.

He glanced around the courtroom as he slowly got to

his feet. There was still no sign of Evan. His eyes touched those of Kathy, of Nacho Newcomb, of Matt himself. Kathy and Nacho were on his side because Evan was, Chadwell knew. And right now they were worried about Evan, just as he was. Matt, meanwhile, was depending on him to save his life.

"Your Honor," Chadwell said, "for my first witness, I call Matt Lindsay to the stand." Without some sort of additional evidence that he had been counting on Evan to produce, there was nothing left to do but put Matt on the stand and let him tell his story.

When Matt had been sworn in, Chadwell said, "Now, Matt, just tell us what happened between you and Johnny Maddock on the night in question."

"Well, sir, we almost got into a gunfight down at the Flores Cantina, just like them other fellas said." Matt was clearly uneasy in the witness chair. "We didn't draw on each other, though. Flores broke it up before it could go that far. Then I went on over to the Double Eagle and did some more drinkin'."

"What happened after that?"

Matt shook his head. "I don't rightly know. Seems like I barely remember leavin' the saloon, but after that it's just a blank until I came to the next mornin' in the doctor's office. I'd been shot." He gestured at the sling that supported his left arm. "Oh, yeah, I had an almighty bad headache, too, and a lump on my head the size of a goose egg."

"Do you remember shooting Johnny Maddock?"

"No, sir, I don't."

Chadwell leaned forward; this was the crucial question. "Matt, do you believe that you shot Johnny?"

Matt slowly shook his head and spoke very clearly. "No, sir. I do not believe that I shot Johnny Maddock."

The door at the back of the courtroom slammed shut. "I know damn well he didn't," Evan said in a voice that filled the room.

He strode in, pandemonium on his heels.

There were gasps of surprise and shouted questions as Evan strode to the defense table. His clothes were torn and bloody, and he looked tired, but there was a fierce grin on his face. Judge Gardner rapped furiously with his gavel as Evan and Chadwell talked rapidly. Evan paused long enough to look over at Kathy, and a special message passed between them as their eyes met. Then he went back to his conference with Chadwell.

When the judge had finally restored order, Howell Trainor was on his feet. "Your Honor, I protest this display! The defense is trying to sway the jury with cheap theatrics!"

Chadwell leaped to his feet to reply. "I apologize for the disturbance, Your Honor," he said. "I can assure the court that there will be no more of what my learned opponent calls cheap theatrics."

"See that there aren't, Counselor," Judge Gardner admonished him. "Well, get on with your case, if you're going to."

"Thank you, Your Honor. No further questions for this witness."

Howell Trainor shook his head. "No questions, Your Honor." There was no point in letting Matt plead his innocence yet again, and it was obvious that was all his case consisted of—his unsupported word.

In the first row behind the prosecution table, Warren Prescott felt as if the floor had dropped out from beneath him. The floor, hell! It felt as if the whole world had gone spinning away. Evan Maddock was alive. He had gotten away from Flores somehow, and if he had captured the cantina owner and brought him back to testify . . .

Prescott started to rise. He could slip out of the courtroom now, maybe steal a horse. He would have to run, but that was better than staying and being exposed as a killer.

"Call your next witness," Judge Gardner said to Chadwell.

Chadwell turned and said, "I call Warren Prescott to the stand."

Prescott froze, every eye on him. He swallowed and forced himself to move, standing up and starting forward as if that was what he had intended all along.

Trainor leaped to his feet again. "Objection, Your Honor! Mr. Prescott has already been called as a prosecution witness. Defense counsel had the opportunity to cross-examine him then."

Chadwell grinned. "I'm not calling him for cross-examination. I'm calling him as a defense witness."

Judge Gardner considered for a moment and then said, "Well, it's irregular, but I'm going to permit it, since this is turning into a most irregular case! Do you have any other surprises up your sleeve, Mr. Chadwell?"

"Just one, Your Honor. With your permission, I'm going to turn over the questioning of this witness to my associate, Evan Maddock."

The judge nodded. "Permission granted."

Evan got to his feet. "I apologize for my appearance, Your Honor," he said as he walked out from behind the table. "I don't normally appear in court this way."

"Just ask your questions, young man."

Prescott was standing beside the witness chair. Every fiber of his being told him to cut and run, but he called on his iron will and made himself grin cockily at Evan. Maybe he could still brazen it out.

He was sworn in and sat down, apparently cool in the stifling heat. Evan looked steadily at him for a moment; no one else in the courtroom was aware of the private battle between these two. They had been enemies from the start, though Evan had only last night discovered that fact, and now it had boiled down to this.

Evan broke the silence by asking, "Where were you three nights ago, Mr. Prescott?"

Prescott frowned and considered. "Three nights ago? I believe I was in my hotel room all evening."

"No, sir, he wasn't!" Gunther Wagner was on his feet in the audience, looking shocked that he had spoken up. He wasn't even sure why he was doing it, other than the fact he knew Prescott was lying.

"Who the devil are *you*?" the judge burst out, glaring at Gunther.

Gunther swallowed nervously. "Uh, my name's Gunther

Wagner, sir. I'm sorry I spoke out of turn. I'll just sit down now."

"No, you won't," Judge Gardner barked. "What were you saying about this witness?"

"Well, sir . . ." Gunther fidgeted a moment, then said, "I saw Mr. Prescott in the alley between the hotel and the stable, sir, so he couldn't have been inside the hotel all night."

"What time was that?" the judge asked.

"About nine o'clock, sir."

Judge Gardner looked back at Evan. "All right, son, go on with your case." He glanced at Howell Trainor. "I know you're aching to object, Mr. Trainor, but don't waste your time. I want to get to the bottom of this, and procedure be hanged."

No one seemed to think that the judge's choice of words was humorous.

Evan stared into Prescott's eyes and asked, "Didn't you pay Cal Ahern to kill my brother Johnny and make it look like Matt Lindsay was the killer?"

"Of course not," Prescott snapped, his face pale now. "That's preposterous."

"And weren't you later forced to murder Cal Ahern to keep him quiet?"

"I've never heard anything so ridiculous—"

"I would remind you that you are under oath, Mr. Prescott."

"I know," Prescott blurted as he nervously stared back and forth between Evan and the table where Howell Trainor sat. "That . . . that doesn't change my answer."

Evan stepped close to the witness chair. "Would your answer remain the same if I told you that Ramirio Flores, owner of the Flores Cantina, is waiting outside this courtroom in the custody of two deputies, charged with attempting to murder me?" He paused momentarily to allow the words to sink in and then continued, "And that he is prepared to back up everything I've said, including the fact that you hired him to dispose of Ahern's body?"

Prescott's face lost its remaining color. His hands shook visibly. "I . . . I d-don't," he sputtered, his wild-eyed gaze swinging to where Kathy Trainor sat. "I m-mean . . ."

"Isn't everything I've said the truth?" Evan pressed. "Didn't you murder Cal Ahern?"

"B-but it had nothing to do with . . . I mean, I had to. He was trying to rob me."

"And didn't you pay Flores to bury him?"

"But just to avoid any publicity," Prescott shot back, his voice taking on a desperate edge. "I had nothing to do with Flores trying to murder you and Ahern's Mexican whore."

"Celestina Morales," Evan said calmly.

"Yes, that's the one."

"Then you know that Flores murdered Celestina Morales?"

"But isn't that what you just said?" Prescott asked.

Evan turned away from the witness chair and walked halfway toward the table where Billy Chadwell and Matt Lindsay were seated. With his back to Prescott, he said in a voice clear enough for all to hear, "I said that Flores tried to murder *me*. I said nothing about him murdering Celestina Morales." Evan turned to face Prescott again. "But you know all about Celestina Morales, because you were there last night . . . because you ordered Flores to murder the two of us. Isn't that true, Mr. Prescott?"

Prescott felt his shoulders droop as the fight went out of him. Staring down, he nodded weakly. Then suddenly he looked up and glared defiantly at Evan. "But it was Ahern and Flores who did the killing. And I'll see that loudmouthed Mexican swine in hell! He'll hang, by god. I'll see that he hangs!"

"No, you won't, Mr. Prescott," Evan replied, "because you can't hang a dead man."

"What?" Prescott muttered, his fingers gripping the arms of the chair.

"I never said that Flores was in custody," Evan continued. "I merely asked what you would say if I *told* you that he was prepared to testify against you. You see, Flores died while I was trying to bring him back to Pecos."

"You mean . . . ?"

"It seems you've convicted yourself, Mr. Prescott."

The courtroom was utterly silent as the truth of Warren Prescott's confession sank in. Then slowly Axel Maddock stood up, pointed a shaking finger at Prescott, and rumbled, "You're the bastard that killed my nephew!"

Jubal Lindsay was on his feet a second later, yelling, "Frame my boy for a killin', will you?"

Chaos exploded again, despite the judge's frantic hammering for order. Warren Prescott leaped to his feet. There was no way out for him; he knew that now. Evan Maddock had beaten him.

But by God, Evan Maddock would die with him!

Prescott grabbed for the derringer concealed beneath his coat. "You won't hang me!" he shouted.

Evan yelled, "No!" He dove across the railing and wrapped his arms around Kathy, throwing her to the floor and shielding her with his body. Chadwell flashed across the aisle and tackled Howell Trainor, to protect him, also. Evan and Chadwell had been raised on the frontier; they knew what was going to happen.

Colts suddenly appeared in the hands of Axel and Jubal. Their men drew the revolvers they had smuggled in, the guns leaping out with blinding speed.

Prescott barely had the derringer out of his coat when they opened up on him. The thunderous barrage of shots lasted only a few seconds, but it seemed a lot longer to the bystanders who were huddled on the floor, where it was safe.

Silence fell over the courtroom again. Judge Leander Gardner looked up over the bench—he had gone diving for cover as well—and surveyed with distaste what was left of Warren Prescott. Evan helped Kathy to her feet and folded her into his arms. She buried her face against his chest so that she wouldn't have to see the gruesome sight. Billy Chadwell got up and offered a hand to the stunned Howell Trainor. Gunther slipped an arm around Mary and held her tightly, while the Maddocks and Lindsays put away their guns in satisfaction. The debt had been settled.

Nacho Newcomb looked over the scene, scratched his head, and said, "He was right. They didn't hang him."

Evan reached up and stroked Kathy's hair in a comforting gesture. He didn't even think about the way she felt in his arms, it seemed so natural. Looking over her shoulder at his grim-faced uncle, he said, "There's something else you might be interested in, Axel. Flores was responsible for the cattle you've been missing, not the Lindsays. In fact, his men are driving the latest bunch south right now. You could pick up their tracks out at that old shack west of town where he tried to kill me."

Axel glared at Evan. "You sure about that, boy?"

"Flores told me about the scheme himself. He was playing you and Jubal against each other." Evan glanced over at Jubal Lindsay, who was a very interested bystander. "Wouldn't surprise me if Flores's men lifted a few head from the Lindsay range, too."

Axel took a deep breath and looked over at Jubal, who returned the cold stare. After a long moment, Axel said gruffly, "Reckon I better go track me down some rustlers." Then he turned and stalked out of the courtroom, his men with him.

Jubal Lindsay said to the shaken Judge Gardner, "You going to hold my boy, Judge?"

Judge Gardner looked pointedly at Warren Prescott's body. "Under the circumstances, all I can say is . . . case dismissed!"

Jubal jerked his head at his son. "Come on, Matt. Be damned if I let a bunch of Maddocks do my work!"

Evan saw Billy Chadwell grinning at him, and Evan couldn't help smiling as well, despite the violence that had rocked the courtroom only moments before.

"It's over," he said softly as he tightened his arms around Kathy. "It's over."

Dusk two days later found Evan leaning on the porch rail of his ranch house once again, but this time he had more company. Kathy Trainor stood beside him, while her father, Billy Chadwell, and Nacho Newcomb sat in the rocking chairs.

It had been a busy two days.

Though Axel Maddock and Jubal Lindsay would deny

it vehemently, they and their men had worked together fairly well in tracking down Flores's men and the stolen cattle. The cattle were back where they belonged now, and there were some unmarked graves along the border trail.

Matt Lindsay and his father had ridden into Pecos the next day, and Matt had effusively thanked Evan and Chadwell for what they had done for him. Jubal Lindsay had even shaken Evan's hand, though he looked a bit pained to be doing such a thing.

Howell Trainor, after pulling himself together, had wired Austin with instructions to begin an investigation of Warren Prescott. If Prescott had been capable of murder, there was no telling what else he might have been involved in. The answers had already started coming back, revealing that Prescott had been a very busy man, setting up payoffs and crooked deals, peddling Trainor's influence without the senator ever being aware of it. Indictments were expected as Prescott's partners in the graft ring were uncovered.

Trainor had been devastated by the news. If he had succeeded in his bid for the governorship and Prescott had still been alive, Prescott would have been a rich man . . . and Trainor would have been nothing but his pawn, a disgrace to the office.

The only part of this whole affair that hadn't been brought to a satisfactory conclusion, as far as Evan was concerned, was Ted. He hadn't spoken to Evan after the trial; instead, he had gone back to the big ranch with Axel.

It looked like he was alone now, Evan thought as he gazed out at the rolling vista of his ranch. But not really alone at all. Kathy was here with him, and he still had his good friends, Billy Chadwell and Nacho. Even Howell Trainor had exhibited a desire to patch things up; he had come to dinner tonight with Kathy, and Chadwell had ridden out from town with them.

Trainor was in an expansive mood after the meal. He lit a cigar and said, "I've been thinking, Evan. Perhaps you should run for office sometime. The people can always use *honest* young men to lead them."

Kathy laughed, a light, happy sound that did things to Evan's heart. "That's what I told him several days ago."

Evan smiled. "Seems to me I've got enough on my plate right now, but maybe someday . . ."

"I believe I'm going to get out of the game when my current term is up. We need some new blood in Austin."

Kathy leaned her head against Evan's shoulder. "I'm glad to hear that, Dad, because I've decided to stay here in Pecos."

Trainor looked surprised for a moment at her announcement. Then he looked at Evan and said, "I'll wager you had something to do with that, Maddock."

Evan grinned and slipped an arm around Kathy. "Damn right I did."

Chadwell lit a cigar of his own and turned to Trainor. "When your term in the senate is over, Howell, you might consider retiring and joining a law firm somewhere, say in a rapidly growing West Texas city. Hell, if Evan takes your advice about politics, I just may be needing a new partner."

Trainor nodded slowly as he considered the idea. "Perhaps," he said. "Perhaps I just might do that."

Nacho stood up. "Riders coming, Evan," he said.

Evan followed the big man's gaze and saw two riders approaching in the gathering gloom. His heart leaped as he recognized them.

Ted and Axel drew rein in front of the porch. Ted slipped down out of the saddle and stood there for a moment, clearly unsure what to do next. Evan met his eyes and felt a lump growing in his throat.

"I want to come back, Evan," Ted said sheepishly. "If you'll have me, that is. Reckon I . . . I had you all wrong."

Evan stepped down off the porch and extended his hand to his brother. "We all had some things wrong," he said.

Ted took his hand, and then Evan pulled him into his arms and hugged him tightly.

Evan looked up and saw Axel glowering down at him. He grinned at the old man. "You still don't like me, do you, Uncle Axel?"

"You still don't act like a proper Maddock, boy, even if you did straighten out that mess."

"Well, if acting like a proper Maddock means acting like a stubborn old bastard, I'm not sure I want to be one. You're still not going to call off that damned feud, are you?"

Axel spat in the dust. "Well, I still ain't got no use for Lindsays, any of 'em. But . . . I guess enough folks have died. If they don't shoot at me, I ain't goin' to shoot at them."

"It's a start, anyway."

Axel wheeled his horse and rode away.

Howell Trainor stood up. "I'd best be getting back to Pecos. I've got a train to catch early in the morning. No more stagecoaches for me, I'm afraid. Gunther and Mary are going to take the coach back to Austin."

Chadwell got to his feet. "I'll ride back in with you, Howell."

Trainor looked at his daughter. "Kathy? Are you coming?"

"Evan and I will ride back in later," she said with a smile.

His arm around Ted's shoulder, Evan rejoined Kathy on the porch. Together, they watched Trainor and Chadwell drive away in the buggy. Nacho stretched and yawned and said, "Believe I'll head on out to the bunkhouse. Good night."

"Good night, Nacho," Evan said.

Evan stood on the porch as the sun vanished behind the faraway mountains, Kathy on one side, Ted on the other, and thought about the brother who wasn't there. He would miss Johnny; the hurt would always be present. But there were good memories, too, and maybe with some work, the legacy of Johnny Maddock would be the end of the long, senseless feud.

But that was something to worry about tomorrow. This day was done.